The Magical
Matchmaker's Legacy

MORNA'S VOW

USA TODAY BESTSELLING AUTHOR
BETHANY CLAIRE

Editor: J.J. Archer
Cover Designed by Sarah Hansen, Okay Creations

Available In eBook, Paperback, & Hardback

eBook ISBN: 978-1-947731-27-1
Paperback ISBN: 978-1-947731-28-8
Hardback ISBN: 978-1-947731-30-1

http://www.bethanyclaire.com

PROLOGUE

Cagair Castle—September 1649

Callum could scarcely see through the billowing smoke. The burning in his lungs made it difficult for him to think as he ran across the lawn to better see what all was aflame. Why did it get hotter the farther he ran from the castle? He spun to see the source of the heat—Orick's old hut—engulfed in flames, the thatch roof quickly disintegrating, the wooden beams creaking as fire consumed them.

Frantic thoughts coursed through his mind until he landed on the one comforting fact he could grasp. None of the servants were here. He'd sent them all away before leaving to join the celebration in the twenty-first century with his family and friends. Thank God for that.

The relief that rushed over him was short-lived. Callum heard a sound so unsettling that he couldn't believe it possible—the screams of a babe. The sound of its cries—screeching, pained, and so frightened—chilled his bones even as heat rose around him.

Callum told himself he only imagined the sounds. He was the only one present at the castle. Then he remembered Tom, the old man from the village who always came up to check on things when Callum was away. He hoped Tom was still at home with his family, that he'd come and gone long before the fire took hold. Surely the screams were only products of his imagination. How could a child be here?

As he ran to escape the cloud of smoke surrounding him, Callum tripped over an object in his path. Before regaining his footing, he screamed, sucking in enough smoke to make his mind swirl. It was Tom in his path. Unconscious and stabbed in his abdomen, the man lay bleeding out onto the grass.

The sound. Callum heard it again. Screaming. Screaming. Over and over. He had to leave Tom and hurry to save the child inside. He couldn't let the smoke overtake him until he saw the babe safe.

In one quick moment of clear thought, he ripped the shirt from his body, tying it quickly over his nose and mouth to prevent some of the smoke from entering his lungs. Not taking a second longer to ponder his choice, he burst into the burning hut and moved blindly toward the sound of the screams.

He found the child quickly. As he reached for the infant, he saw two others in the haze, both clearly dead from inhaling the smoke. That same deadly threat would most likely take his life in a few short moments. He just hoped he could see the child safely outside and that, by some miracle, the babe would live.

Callum exited the hut and managed to run with the child far beyond the smoke before a sudden pain in his leg sent him to his knees. He let loose of the infant, hoping it landed far enough away that the flames wouldn't reach it. His leg was on fire, and the pain pushed away any clear thought. He rolled and swung until the fire consuming him extinguished, but the pain made everything around him spin.

Save magic, nothing would stop the fire from spreading, and he wasn't a sorcerer by any stretch of the imagination.

Unconsciousness threatened to overtake him, whether from smoke or pain, he didn't know. Just as he began to surrender to it, rain poured down upon his face, a great gush of it. Panicked, Callum threw himself over the child to keep her from drowning.

Lifting his head, he saw her—a woman. Old and cloaked, she stood with outstretched arms, as if she summoned the storm from willpower alone.

The fire surrendered, and so did Callum, closing his eyes as he held the baby against him.

CHAPTER 1

Cagair Castle—March 1650—Six Months Later

"Ye must stop crying, Jane," said Callum. "I know ye love her, as do I. Adwen could not even stand to be here he was so saddened to see her go, but she is not ours. Ye've done well by her, but ye must stop crying before Laird Allen's brother arrives. Please. Ye are breaking my heart."

Sobbing, Jane held baby Nora as tightly as she could. The baby cried right along with her. No matter how hard he tried not to, Callum found himself crying as well at the thought of seeing the wee girl go.

"I...I know she's not mine by birth, but she is mine now," cried Jane. "No one is ever going to love her as much as I do. She's mine in every way that matters. What is Laird Allen's brother going to do with her? We don't know anything about him. He could be awful. Most likely he will just hand her off to be raised by some of his servants. Just ask him, Callum. That's all I want. If you don't, I will, and we both know the sort of impression I tend to make on people of this time."

He wrapped his arms around his sister-in-law, squeezing her in comfort as he watched the newest laird of the Allen's territory crest the hill and ride up the narrow, high path leading to Cagair. It was a sad day for them all, but for none more so than Jane. Unable to have children of her own, she had claimed Nora the day after the fire.

"Aye, fine. I'll speak to him. Here, lass." He pulled out a cloth he'd tucked inside the waist of his kilt for safekeeping and dabbed away at Jane's face. "He's nearly here."

Jane sniffed. "What has taken him so long to get here, anyway? It's been six months, Callum."

"He was not even in the country. It took months for anyone to track him down. Ye canna blame his late arrival on his not caring. We doona know that."

Callum wasn't acquainted with any of the Allens. While owners of the single largest territory in all of Scotland, their land lay so far north that they remained isolated from most of the rest of the country. Even as well traveled as he was, Callum had never visited their territory. It still shocked him that Laird Allen and his wife had arrived at his home so unexpectedly, and on the one day he was not there to keep them safe.

Many more men accompanied Raudrich Allen than Callum had anticipated. He hoped that didn't mean the new laird was out to avenge the one responsible for his brother's death.

Motioning for Jane to stay back, Callum walked toward Raudrich Allen, breathing a sigh of relief as the man smiled gently and nodded to him in greeting.

"Laird MacChristy, I am pleased to finally meet ye, though I do wish 'twas not after such tragedy."

Callum waited for Raudrich to dismount then extended a hand toward him. "I, as well. Ye canna know how sorry I am for what happened. Had I known they were coming, I never would have left the castle. I would have made certain we had protections in place."

Although Raudrich looked to be older than Callum, he thought them to be about the same age. The sun had weathered Raudrich beyond his years.

"O'course ye would've." Raudrich nodded. "Ye bear no responsibility. Accidents happen no matter where we find ourselves. My brother and his wife knew that as well as anyone. They planned to return home before their child was born, but an early labor saw fit to change their plans."

Callum couldn't imagine how news of the truth about the fire had yet to reach Raudrich. It had been no accident.

"Laird Allen, do ye not know what happened here?" Callum asked. "I am verra sorry that ye have not learned before now. The fire was set on purpose."

"No. That canna be."

Callum could see from Raudrich's expression that it was indeed the first time he'd heard such news.

"We dinna know for certain for some weeks, but 'twas Laird Macaslan. The old man who watches over the castle when I'm gone was stabbed after the fire was set. Macaslan left him for dead, but Tom survived. When he woke, we learned what truly happened."

Laird Allen reached out to lean against his horse for support. Callum knew how the news must feel to him. An accidental fire was one thing, but an act of violence was another.

Raudrich heaved a troubled sigh. "What did happen, then?"

"Tom was here when yer brother and his family arrived. He was just about to see them inside when he spotted Macaslan's men approaching. He knew of the ill will between Macaslan and myself and told yer family to hide in the hut. He couldn't stop Macaslan and his riders from setting the castle afire, but hoped they would leave the outer building alone. They might have if not for the babe's screaming. Macaslan set fire to the hut immediately, not wanting any witnesses to his crimes. Then he stabbed Tom, leaving him for dead. I arrived back after Macaslan and his men had already departed. The only one I could save was the babe."

He still couldn't speak of that night without choking up. Raudrich reached out to place a hand on his shoulder. "Thank ye for saving the child. I canna bear to think of her being lost."

Callum was glad, as well, but it wasn't nearly enough. If not for him, the child's parents would still be alive. "So ye see, Laird Allen, 'twas not an accident that killed yer kin. No one is to blame but me."

"No one?" Laird Allen scowled. "I'd say Macaslan is the one to blame, lad. What did ye do to anger him?"

"I prevented his son from marrying a lass that dinna want him —a lass that already belonged to another."

"Ah. That is not enough reason for a man to burn yer home and property. This was not yer doing, Callum. We must see Macaslan dead."

Callum couldn't agree more. If only the wretch would return to Scotland. "Aye, though he's not been seen since the night of the fire. His son holes up in their castle, and his father has fled the country. We've eyes on nearly every shore. When he sees fit to return, we'll know."

"Where do ye think he's gone? My men willna be returning home until we've seen Macaslan's head separated from his body. If ye are watching for him to return, we will go seek him out."

Callum was sure that most of Scotland felt the same. He couldn't think of any possible ally for Macaslan. More clans than not had been wronged by him in some way or another.

"A merchant in Macaslan's territory claims he has friends in Spain, though I doona know if he would travel so far," Callum said.

"To Spain we will go then." For the first time, Raudrich acknowledged Jane and gestured toward the child in her arms.

"How is the babe? Have ye named her? I doona know what my brother called the lass."

Jane approached them then; Callum was not surprised she refused to remain in the background where he'd left her.

"Nora," Jane said, her gaze lowered to the baby's face. "I call her Nora."

"'Tis a lovely name," Laird Allen said softly. "Can I see her?"

Callum watched Jane closely, hoping with his every breath that she wouldn't turn and bolt toward the portal with the child in tow. She trembled all over, but slowly she handed the baby over to Laird Allen. Nora started to scream immediately.

Raudrich held the baby away from him awkwardly, baring his teeth as he spoke over the baby's cry. "She looks much like her mother. She doesna seem to care for me much."

Jane's voice, weepy and cracked, answered, "You...you have to hold her closer to you."

Laird Allen nodded but continued to hold the child away from him. "Aye, I'm sure. What is yer name, lass? Are ye Callum's wife?"

"No." Both he and Jane said simultaneously. Embarrassed, Callum stepped back, allowing Jane to lead the conversation.

"No. I'm Jane, Adwen's wife. Adwen is Callum's brother."

Laird Allen nodded once again and continued to stare at the baby with apprehension. "Do ye love her, Jane?"

Callum feared Jane would rip the child from his arms at any moment. When she answered, her voice was filled with emotion. "Very much."

"I can see that. Why doona ye keep her? All the babe's parents would want is for her to be loved. I would love her, but a babe needs more than what I have to give her, aye? I'm not married, and from the sounds of it, I'll be headed to Spain soon. I canna care for the child like ye can."

Jane stepped forward and gleefully took Nora back into her arms. "Do you mean it? If you say I can keep her, I need your word that you will not want her back. It nearly killed me handing her to you just then. I couldn't say goodbye to her again."

Laird Allen turned his back to them, said a quick word to his men, and mounted his horse. "Aye, lass. I will rest easy knowing that Nora will grow up with a mother who loves her just as much as her birth mother did. I'll not take up any more of yer time. My men will see my family's remains safely back to our home. I'll be in search of Laird Macaslan, and I'll be in touch with ye soon, Callum."

Callum stood beside Jane, watching until their visitor rode out of sight. Then Jane threw one of her arms around Callum, squishing Nora in between them hard enough to elicit an unhappy scream from the babe.

"Thank you. Thank you, thank you, thank you, thank you, thank you, Callum."

He stared at her incredulously, turning to lead them both back to the portal. "Why are ye thanking me? I dinna do it. Laird Allen did."

"But you saved her, and she's become my world. I am grateful to Laird Allen, too, but I mean, seriously, what's wrong with him? Who gives their niece over to a total stranger like that? For all he knows, he could have just given her over to a complete nut-job."

Callum laughed. "I believe he just did," he teased.

Jane gave him a quick nudge in the ribs with her elbow before sprinting ahead of him and down the staircase portal.

He knew as he followed her into the twenty-first century that this would be the happiest day they'd all had in many, many months.

CHAPTER 2

taly—Present Day

The sound of sneakers on cobblestone streets always soothed me in a way that little else could. It meant that the rest of the world, or at least everyone in my tiny village, still slept. For those few, precious, forty-odd minutes, all that mattered was the sound of my feet against the ground and the steady rhythm of my own labored breathing. This was the only time of day that I kept for myself. Even with the chest cold I had this morning, I refused to miss out on my run.

As a child, I spent my summers in the restaurant helping my grandmother in whatever manner she allowed, watching her with a dreamlike admiration that distorted my memories in a way I could only see now. While working in the kitchen and serving up three meals daily to the town's residential regulars, she'd been vibrant, energetic, and alive. My grandmother made everyone around her smile. You could taste her love in every meal she cooked, and all I ever wanted was to be just like her.

But away from her restaurant, in the small home where she spent her life, she was so tired she fell asleep the moment she sat down. So out of touch with anything outside of her restaurant, she could talk of little else. As a young girl, I always thought that the restaurant was the source of all her energy—a light in her life that she loved so much that time away from it pained her. Perhaps if I'd spent more than those few weeks each summer with her, I would have seen the truth. She loved her work, that much was true, but the restaurant was a vacuum to her soul until the day she died. It took her energy, her focus, her time, and any chance she ever had at real happiness.

I could see all of that now. I could see it because I experienced it firsthand. While my grandmother allowed work to rule her life, I refused to do so. Mr. Abbiati would be shocked if I landed another job—he had no idea I was even looking—but I knew he'd noticed how run down I'd become, even if he chose to ignore it for the sake of his business.

I let out a frustrated sigh as I rounded the last corner of my run. The breath caught uncomfortably in my chest, sending me into a fit of coughing that told me I had no real business cooking for anyone today. Still, I knew that I would. There was no one to help me, and lots of locals would be mighty upset if I closed without notice. I stopped running just outside the restaurant door, hurrying to find my key so I could go inside for a glass of water to soothe my cough.

"You sound terrible."

I gasped and started at the voice, dropping the keys. In my three years of running the restaurant, I'd never encountered another soul while out on my early morning run. Mr. Abbiati spoke Italian, as did everyone here, but I unthinkingly answered him in English, gripping my chest as I caught my breath and bent to pick up the keys I'd dropped.

"Oh, you scared me." I caught my mistake and continued in Italian. "What are you doing up this early, Mr. Abbiati?"

He often stopped in during the day to check on me and visit over a cup of coffee, but never this early in the day.

"I'm always up this early, but it's not often that I'm out of the house until after the sun is up. I don't ever sleep, really. I was reading by my window and saw you run by. I thought Francesca and I would meet you at the end of your run for an early morning coffee. I need to talk to you."

I glanced down at Francesca, taking notice of the leashed cat for the first time. Perhaps many cats are accustomed to being walked around on a leash, but the only one I'd ever seen was Francesca, a cat so dog-like that she never failed to put a smile on my face. Mr. Abbiati never went anywhere without her.

"Of course, come on in. I'll get us some coffee and Francesca some milk. Do you mind visiting with me while I look over my emails? I need to track my latest seafood order."

He nodded and followed me inside, sitting quietly down at the small table inside the kitchen where I often rested between meal rushes. It didn't take long to brew the coffee. After preparing it just the way Mr. Abbiati liked, I squeezed his shoulder and sat down beside him, opening up my laptop to check on the order.

"I'm worried about you, Sydney," he said. "I have been for some time."

"Oh?" In truth, I was only half listening to him. While tracking my order, another email at the top of my inbox captured my attention. Nearly six months had passed since I'd submitted an application for the job, and I'd long since let the dream of it go. To see a response from Cagair Castle in Scotland after all of this time astonished me completely.

"Yes. You've aged far more in three years than any young woman as healthy as you should. You're already far too invested in this place. If you don't intervene on behalf of your own sanity soon, you will lose yourself to it. I care too much for you to allow that to happen."

"Uh-huh." Now I definitely wasn't listening, for the first

sentence in the message had my heart beating so fast I might as well have still been running. This was it. The change I needed. It didn't matter to me that the job wasn't officially mine. A shot at it gave me the confidence to make the choice I had pondered for so long.

"Sydney, are you listening to me?"

Taking a breath to slow my pulse and build my courage, I closed my computer and looked over at my boss. "No. I'm sorry. I wasn't. I just got some news that I need to share with you. What were you saying?"

I could see that I'd frustrated him. He crossed his arms in a way meant to show me just how unhappy he was. "It doesn't matter. You're fired, Sydney."

"I'm quitting, Mr. Abbiati."

We had spoken at the exact same time. Smiling, I pointed at him, then leaned back in my chair and crossed my arms to mimic his stance. "You first. You're firing me? Why?"

"Well, I guess I'm not if you're quitting. Though I must say I'm glad to hear it. I didn't want to fire you, but I was ready to do it."

I shook my head, confused. "Again. Why?"

"Your grandmother, Sydney. I loved her for more than forty years, and I know she loved me as much as she was capable. I'd have married her if she would have let me. But, alas, she could never pull away from this place long enough to build a life for herself. I don't want that to happen to you. I know she wouldn't want it for you, either."

"Neither do I." I didn't know what else to say to him. I imagined we were both very much in shock that we were on the same page. That rarely happened.

"You're far braver than she was. Leaving this job proves that. Your grandmother knew everyone, but she knew no one. She knew names and faces of countless people but understood too little of herself to know the heart or mind of any other. It's an empty life to live that way, and it brings nothing but pain to those who love a person who has lost herself to something that doesn't matter. Not to say that hard work doesn't matter, it does, but only if you know who and what you're working for. Working for work's sake gets you nowhere. That is precisely how Elizabetta spent her life."

Tears sprang up in my eyes. I couldn't tell if they were due to relief or the sad memory of my grandmother's life.

He didn't wait for me to respond. "So. Tell me about this new job."

"Well, it's not actually mine yet, but it will be after I show them how great I am. It's in Scotland."

"Scotland, huh? Well, at least you won't be torturing the rest of us with your awful Italian anymore."

I shook my head at him. My Italian was perfect, and everyone in the village knew it.

"Yes, it's at a castle that was very recently renovated. They're turning it into a luxury resort. It's a bit strange, though. I applied so long ago, and I just got the response this morning."

He threw back the rest of his coffee and reached to pour himself more. "What did it say?"

"Just that if I wanted to come to the castle for a test run, they would interview me and make a decision on my employment then. Don't worry, though, I won't leave until I find my replacement."

I hoped such a task wouldn't take long. If it were possible, I would've left on the spot.

CHAPTER 3

agair Castle—Present Day

aily sessions with Morna were a painful necessity to Callum's healing. Both he and baby Nora came to the witch's temporary bedchamber at the castle each night to be treated for their damaged lungs and the hideous burn that ran down his thigh. Morna's magic helped. Slowly, day by day, things were getting easier for the two of them.

He always enjoyed holding the little girl, and he found that Jane handed her over a little more easily now that she knew the babe was hers forever. Despite her tragic start in life, Nora was a happy child. Bouncing her on his hip as he hobbled toward Morna's room, Callum laughed when Nora pulled gently on his earlobes. He knocked at Morna's door, but didn't bother waiting for a response before entering the room. He knew she'd be expecting them the same as always.

"Good evening, Morna. How is my favorite witch?" he teased.

She smiled at him, but it was an uneasy smile, and he immediately regretted his joke. For a moment, he'd forgotten Morna's uneasiness about what he'd witnessed at Cagair the night of the fire.

"I'm yer only witch," she said.

"Aye, that ye are."

"Now bring the babe here. I want to kiss her cheeks."

He handed Nora over to her, moving to gather the herbs and potions that Morna used on them nightly.

"She seems in a verra good mood today, does she not, Callum? Do ye think she knows that she's staying with Jane and the thought pleases her?"

He wondered the same thing. While always pleasant, Nora seemed to glow today. "If anything, I think she sees that Jane is no longer so stressed about giving her up, and Jane's happiness makes her happy." He studied the old woman for a moment. "What of ye, Morna? Ye look as if Jane's worry has transferred over to ye."

"Aye, I believe it has. I'm worried about Jerry."

Last he'd seen Jerry, the old man seemed fine. Concerned, Callum asked, "What's happened to him? Is he all right?"

"Aye, for now. It's his heart. He's not cared for it the way he should, and it's dangerously close to becoming a real problem for him. I can see it, but he willna let me work on him with magic. 'Tis a promise I made him long ago."

"Why? He must know that if ye are worried, there's reason for him to allow ye to do whatever ye will with yer powers."

Morna huffed. "Aye, he should, but he's a stubborn old fool."

"Would ye like me to talk to him? I doona know if he will listen, but I can try."

Morna reached for his arm and pulled him fully inside, shutting the door. "Aye, but first let's get on with the babe's treatment before she loses her smile."

Callum helped balance the little girl on the small table so Morna could rub the soothing oils on her back; Nora had grown so used to the procedure she rarely even fussed anymore.

"How many more times do ye think she needs this?" Callum asked.

Morna shrugged as she leaned in to listen to Nora's breathing. "Not many more. Maybe another week. She's healing nicely. Ye have as well." Looking up at him, the old woman narrowed her eyes. "Callum, can I ask ye something?"

"Of course." It was unlike Morna to ask permission for anything. Her hesitation made him curious.

"The witch ye saw on the day of the fire...I know 'twas many months ago now, but do ye remember anything of the way she looked? Could ye describe her to me at all?"

He remembered well. Even as he'd lost consciousness from the pain in his leg and the smoke in his lungs, she had stood out to him like the sun on a cloudless day. If not for her, he knew much more of his beloved castle would have been lost.

"Aye." Callum nodded. "She was tall—as tall as many men—and quite thin. She had both hands extended toward the sky, and her nails were pointed and sharp. Her hair was grayed with just a few streaks of black still remaining. She was old, mayhap the oldest person I've ever seen."

Callum had never before seen such worry or fear in Morna's eyes. He didn't miss how she swallowed hard before she spoke.

"Aye. She would be old, far older than anyone has a right to be."

"Do you know her? Why would ye not have mentioned this before?" Callum had searched for the witch twice since the fire, and each time he had failed to find her.

"I'm sorry, Callum. I dinna want it to be true that it was her, though deep down, I knew it must've been. The thought frightened me. I dinna want ye to find her. I've felt her here at Cagair this time; her presence was never palpable until now. I thought her dead until ye told me yerself what happened at the fire."

Callum felt a deep foreboding. "Who is she? What does she mean to ye?"

"If I tell ye, ye must keep it to yerself. Not a soul knows it, save me and Jerry."

Lifting baby Nora into his arms, he swore his secrecy.

"Her name is Grier," Morna said after a long hesitation. "The last time Jerry and I saw her, I was eighteen years old."

Startled, Callum said, "Do ye mean…ye canna mean that Jerry has been to yer time—the time ye were born in, not just this one?" He couldn't imagine it. As uncomfortable as Jerry was around magic, he couldn't imagine him traveling through time.

"Aye, but 'twas not his choice to do so. He doesna speak of it, so doona ask him about it."

Callum watched Morna closely. "Ye seem frightened of this Grier. Did she harm ye or Jerry?"

"No." Morna shook her head. "She did me no harm. I left her before she could. But, aye, I am frightened of her. She's not been at Cagair for ages, but her power over the portal here remained. It's why I thought she was dead. It's changed now. Not only because of what she did with the fire. Normally, I doona have power here. Now I do."

Oftentimes, Morna made the habit of speaking of her powers and magic as if everyone else understood, though most did not.

"I doona know what ye mean, Morna," Callum told her. "What kept ye from having yer powers before?"

Morna motioned for him to sit down on the workbench so she could take to healing his leg. "When a witch dies, we can root our powers to one place, or to a person if we so choose. It means that even after our death, whatever spells we cast there remain. Whatever our realm, it canna be touched by another with power. What I dinna know was that one can leave their power in a place even if they are not dead, and then come back to claim it another time."

Callum lifted his brows. "So that is what this Grier has done?"

"Aye. She's reclaimed her power. I know because her realm is no longer protected, allowing me to perform magic here as well. Though she's kept the portal open even after returning, I doona think it bodes well for any of us."

Frowning, Callum asked, "What ill will would she have toward any of us? If she wished to cause us harm, why would she have stopped the fire that day?"

"Callum, Cagair was Grier's home. Technically, no matter yer claim, I suppose in her mind it still is. She would want to protect it." Morna lifted her eyes to his. "If she's back, it's for me."

He would have to continue the search for this witch. With Macaslan's wrath still lingering, he had enough threats facing his loved ones. Callum couldn't allow anyone else the opportunity to hurt those near him ever again.

"What does she want with ye?" he asked. "If it's to hurt ye, I'll find and kill her. I swear it."

"No, I doona want ye near her," Morna blurted "She willna hurt me. Nor do I think she'd truly hurt anyone else. Grier will wish to speak to me, though, and I doona know just what she'll do to get me to go back." She sighed. "I canna go back, Callum. Not ever. Ye canna know how painful it is for me to even think of it."

Nora started to cry. With Morna finished treating his leg, Callum handed the baby over to her. The old woman started to rock to and fro, and he hoped the motion would soothe Morna's nerves as well as the babe's.

"Then doona go back," he said to her. "Ignore the witch. If she's harmless, let her do her worst to interfere with things. We're all fairly used to the unexpected by now. Is it possible she would come forward?"

Morna shook her head in response to him. "No. I doona think she would. But Callum, ye best take back what ye just said. If ye doona think she listens in even now, ye are a fool. She's a tricky witch if I've ever known one. Doona tempt her to mess with yer life. If ye do, ye can be sure she'll take ye up on the challenge."

Callum waved off the warning. "Morna, so much has happened these last months, the last thing I'm worried about is a witch as harmless as ye. I'd rather her do what she wishes with me than with anyone else."

"I dinna ever say she was harmless, lad," said Morna, her tone harsh and cool. "Ye are the one that said that. I simply meant I doona think she would kill anyone outright. There's a fair difference between harmless and a murderer, would ye not say? Ye'd do good to remember it."

CHAPTER 4

*I*taly

*W*ithin a week, Mr. Abbiati lined up three web interviews for the two of us, and they were all excellent candidates to take my place at the restaurant. In the end, Mr. Abbiati chose a rather serious student a few years younger than me. Mark spoke Italian fluently and seemed to have the sort of temperament I believed would mesh well with the locals.

My favorite thing about my replacement was that he was as eager to take over the job as I was to leave it. He planned to arrive the next day for a quick afternoon training session with me. Then I would be free.

I slipped away in the late afternoon to draw up his employment papers. The task didn't take me long. Just as I was about to shut off the computer, a familiar and friendly face popped up on the screen—my little sister, Liv. It was only then that I realized I'd yet to tell my family the big news. By my calculations, Liz should've still been in school. Not that it mattered to me; I would never dream of chiding her for calling me.

I smiled as I clicked the green *Accept* button, eager to see her smiling little face.

"Hey, Liv. I miss you." And I did. Every day. She'd be nine in a month, and I hated that I'd missed so much of her life during the past three years. I hoped that my work schedule wouldn't be as strenuous once I landed the job in Scotland, and I would be able to travel back home to see her more often.

Liv beamed at me. "I miss you, too. Whatcha doing? I'm surprised you answered."

Truthfully, I was surprised, too. Not that I would deny her call if I saw it, but her timing couldn't have been more perfect. She'd caught me during the five minutes out of the entire day that I could have even seen her call.

"I just sat down for a few minutes," I told my sister. "I'll have to check on some things that are cooking soon."

"Yeah, I knew you'd be busy, but I had a dentist appointment this morning and got to miss school!"

Liv's smile always squeezed my heart in a way that made me want to jump on the first plane back home. She'd been the happiest surprise that my parents and I ever received. I only wished that I hadn't already moved out of their home when she arrived.

"Well that's nice," I said, "but I've never seen anybody so excited to go to the dentist."

She blew air through her lips in dismissal. "I don't know why people don't like the dentist. It's fun. I'm going to have to go back to school in just a few minutes, but Mom said I could call you real fast and say *hi*."

"Well, I am so glad you did. It's actually really good that you called because I have some big news for all of you." I paused. "Is Dad home?"

"Nope. He's still at work. You want me to get Mom?"

"Yes, please." I waited patiently as she ran to get our mother, and I smiled when both of their faces appeared on the screen.

"Hey, Sydney." Mom sent me a curious smile. "You look good, much better than you have in a long time. What's going on? Is there a boy?"

"No, Mom. No boy. It's much better than that. I quit my job."

My mother and my sister stared back at me, their mouths open. I decided to fill them in with the rest of the news before they got their hopes up that I was coming back to the States.

"I'm moving to Scotland for a job there. It's in a castle!" I tried to convey my enthusiasm. When they both smiled, my nerves abated a little.

"Scotland!" Liv's voice rang with excitement. "You love castles, right?"

I smiled and nodded in agreement. "Who doesn't?"

She shrugged, chuckling just the tiniest bit. "Well, I bet anyone who got thrown into the dungeon of a castle doesn't. But you're not going to be in the dungeon, so I say *awesome*."

I laughed and nodded. "I say awesome, too. What do you think, Mom?" There was a bit of delay with the signal so it took a few seconds for me to see that she was crying. "Mom? What's wrong? I thought you'd be happy." She had never liked the idea of me working in her mother's restaurant.

She swiped at her eyes. "I am so happy, I feel I might burst. Will you have to work as much?"

"I don't think so, and I'm going to tell them right away that I have to be able to go home for Christmas, or I won't do it."

"That's wonderful," Mom said. "Maybe we can come visit you, Sydney. I would love to see a real castle."

I wanted nothing more than for them to jump on a plane that instant. "I would love that. And as long as you tell Dad that you'll let him quote *Braveheart* to his heart's content, I bet he won't mind either."

My mother spoke between sniffles. "I...I would love that, too."

"Great, then let's plan on it. I need to check on a few things in the kitchen, but I'll talk to you soon. I love you both so much."

They told me goodbye, and I shut down my computer before gleefully walking back to the restaurant. If only tomorrow would hurry up and arrive. I was certain that, until time came for me to actually leave, I would doubt the reality of any of what I'd set into motion.

CHAPTER 5

agair Castle—Present Day

Only after Morna's mention of it could Callum see the recent decline in Jerry's health—the way he slept in the early afternoon, the way he slouched in his chair while awake, and the fatigue that etched every crevice of his friend's face. Simply helping Callum clean out the chicken coop tired him, and that wasn't like Jerry. Neither were the spells of dizziness he thought no one noticed. Callum knew Jerry tried his best to hide from everyone what was happening to him.

"Ye see what I mean, doona ye?" Morna whispered.

Callum stood at the corner of the sitting room. He'd been on his way to speak with Jerry as he told Morna he would, only to find Jerry snoring by the fire. It didn't surprise him when Morna walked up.

"Aye, I see. Do ye wish me to wake him, or speak with him another time?"

"Another time. Come." Morna gave him a gentle nudge with her elbow. "Let's allow him to sleep until dinner."

Lacing his arm with Morna's, he led her out into the hallway. It seemed so strange to him that after months of living alone at the Cagair of his own time, he would be living with so many friends and family members now.

Baby Nora's survival and presence among them was the one blessing of that wretched fire, but Macaslan's act of violence proved to him just how fortunate he was to have such selfless friends with large families—all of whom were familiar with the magic hidden throughout Scotland.

His uncle, Donal MacChristy, the rather more responsible counterpart to his father, had been the first to arrive with his men. To everyone's surprise, Donal had placed spies within Macaslan's territory the moment he learned of the laird's ransom of Callum's father and brother. Through his spies, Donal learned of Macaslan's plan to set fire to Cagair. Unfortunately, the news came too late. He'd been unable to arrive in time, showing up just after Callum lost consciousness in the rain. Still, they all knew that without Donal, things would have turned out very differently. It was only through Donal's men that they knew Macaslan had boarded a boat to an unknown destination after calls for his head began to reverberate throughout all of the country.

Only through Donal's intelligence did they know it was safe to gather and work to repair Cagair. For if Macaslan had remained in Scotland, Callum would never have allowed the rest of his friends and family to join him at at the castle, leaving their own homes and territories weakened and open to Macaslan's threat.

Morna and Jerry were the first to arrive at the Cagair of the twenty-first century, with Morna eager to use her powers on the wee babe the moment she learned of what happened.

The McMillans, with their connection to Cagair already formed through the young lad Cooper and his aunt Jane, arrived next. The Conalls, his distant cousins through marriage, arrived shortly behind them, providing a good number of men to help rebuild Cagair.

With the stairwell portal an easy way to get back and forth across the centuries, everyone piled into the Cagair that existed in a time ahead of his own. Each day, he and the other men would travel through to his own time to meet with hired men for work on the castle. Each night, they would come back through to meet with their wives and children in the evenings. Their progress was slow, but everything was much better than it had been a few months ago—a sweet reminder to all of them that time could change so much.

"How did work go today?" Morna asked, pulling him from his thoughts.

"It went verra well. The bedchambers in the right wing have been set right, though the furnishings are not complete. We've dozens of women in the village working diligently to create the necessary bedding, draperies, and candles. I owe so much to my people and to all of ye who have come here."

"We all owe much to ye as well, Callum. Even if we are all crammed in this castle so tightly that we trip over each other in the hallways, I think everyone enjoys being together verra much. I know I do. There are so many here that I thought I would never see again. Why, I wish I'd had my camera out when Donal came through the portal for the first time."

Callum laughed, remembering his uncle's reaction to everything. For all of them, the miracles of the twenty-first century never seemed to cease. Each day provided something new to discover.

"I've enjoyed it as well," Callum admitted. "I'm ready to have my castle back, though."

"Aye. I know ye are. How much longer before ye are finished? I'll be glad for it as well. Every moment that everyone is gathered here, no matter how fun and joyous, I fear Grier's meddling."

Callum had thought little of the witch the past few days. He couldn't see the point in Morna's worry. As far as he could tell, Grier intended to remain at a distance. Otherwise, why wouldn't she have allowed him to find her after the fire?

Turning to look at Morna as they walked, he said, "I expect it to take another full turning of the moon, mayhap a few weeks more. As long as nothing sets us back."

"Hmm..."

Morna's apprehensive noise said more than her words ever could. "Morna...do ye have reason to believe something will?"

The witch shrugged, pulling away from his arm as she sat down at the top of the castle's main staircase. "No. 'Tis only a feeling. Grier had already started whatever she wishes to do. Just ye wait and see."

A memory flashed in his mind, something he'd wished to ask Morna about long ago. "Can I ask ye something about the magic here, Morna? I know 'tis not yer doing, but I wondered if mayhap ye know how it works."

Morna laughed quietly, and he could see with her every sarcastic gesture just how much everything bothered her lately.

"Clearly, I doona understand a thing about the magic here, since I thought she was dead all this time." She sighed. "But please, ask me yer question. I'll tell ye what I can."

He sat down beside her. "I suppose ye know how we all discovered the portal, aye? Cooper put it all together. When the rest of us thought we were seeing ghosts, he knew we were seeing mirages of those ahead of us."

"Aye. I remember. He looked for it so he could find me. He hoped that I would heal Isobel. While I thought it a mistake, I am glad she still lives. What of it?"

Callum nodded, thinking back on that time at Cagair when they'd all grown so close to the kind Isobel and her husband. He missed her often. Once all was well within his own time, he would make a trip with Adwen and Jane to see her.

"I often saw what I thought were ghosts here," Callum

explained. "Always the same people—three women and a man. I know now who three of them are, but I've never seen the fourth."

"Well, who are the three?"

"Gillian, Anne, and Aiden. I always saw the fourth one in my bedchamber. Her black hair is so beautiful, her eyes so piercing, I found I rather fancied her—ghost or not. But when I came through for the first time—when I met with those I'd seen—I couldna make sense of why this lass was not amongst them. How can it be so? Do ye think she truly was a ghost?"

He must have stumped Morna, for they sat in silence next to each other for a long while as he watched her ponder his question. When she finally looked up at him, anger shone in her eyes, and he suspected her answer even before she gave it.

"'Tis Grier, clearly. Not the lass ye saw, but Grier is the one who showed her to ye. Ye are also the one who saw Grier at the fire. I can see it now—'tis yer life she means to mess with. I told ye not to tease her the other day. If I was a wagering woman—which I only am with Jerry—I'd wager that ye will see this lass soon."

He rather hoped that he would. Everyone around him had someone they loved deeply. Why shouldn't it be his turn to have a go at things? "Do ye think so?"

Morna stood and crossed her arms as she waited for him to do the same. When he joined her, she turned her back to him, walking away as she spoke. "Aye, ye will, I'm sure of it. And, Callum, once ye do...doona trust the lass for a second."

CHAPTER 6

*I*taly

While I thought time would drag due to my excitement, everything came about quickly once Mark arrived. He was a saint in the kitchen. Even after only one afternoon of him cooking, I could tell everyone in the village would be madly in love with him by the end of the week. His arrival and total competence in the kitchen left me confident I could leave my job feeling entirely guilt-free.

On the morning of my flight, with everything ready to go and loaded into the back of my car, I stopped in at Mr. Abbiati's one last time. I expected him to be sad to see me go. Instead, he could hardly contain his readiness for me to leave.

"Go ahead, Sydney." He gestured to the door. "Get out of here. You'll be late."

It was five hours until my flight, and I only had an hour drive to the airport. Even if I lingered around for two more hours, I wasn't likely to be late.

"No, I won't be," I insisted. "I'm way ahead of schedule, and I'm never late."

He laughed and clicked his teeth. "Oh, you just ruined it for yourself. You'll certainly be late now that you tested fate that way. Get on. Go."

I smiled and moved in to hug him. "What's the matter with you? I thought you'd be at least a little sad for me to leave." I sounded rather juvenile, I knew, but I wanted someone to miss me.

"Sydney. . . " He sighed. "I'm worried that if you linger too long you will talk yourself out of going, and that would be crazy. Do they know you're coming?"

I was fairly certain that I wouldn't talk myself out of going, but after all these years, I understood why he thought that I might. "Well, the email said to just stop by, so that's what I'm going to do. I'm all about spontaneity now."

He frowned as he ushered me out of his house and into the street where my car was running. "You should call them, just to let them know you're on your way."

"Fine, I'll call them during my layover in Paris." I opened the driver's side door and lowered myself into the car where I started to tell him goodbye, only to have him slam the door in my face mid-sentence. Smiling, he waved me on so that I would leave. I'd never felt so unwanted in my life.

Eagair Castle—Present Day

"What are you doing back here so early?"

Callum reached for an apple on the counter before turning to address Anne's question. She stood at the other end of the island, covered in flour. She looked like she was about to scream—or maybe cry; he could never really tell with Anne.

"I'm not early. 'Tis nearly nightfall. All of us are back. I just doona have a wife or children wanting my attention, so I can ready myself for dinner more quickly than the others. Do ye need some help?"

He didn't know what he could do to assist her, but even he was likely more apt in the kitchen than Anne. He admired her determination, though. No matter how bad her meal was the night before, she always took another stab at feeding them the next evening. Still, he feared their clothes were beginning to hang off them more loosely.

"Well..."

Just as she was about to answer him, the telephone on the opposite side of the kitchen rang. Callum was only vaguely familiar with phones, and their noise made him jump every time. He'd never heard this phone ring once in all the months he'd been here.

Anne brushed her hands together to remove the flour and made her way over to the telephone. "Well, that's weird. I didn't even know that worked. Give me just a second."

He nodded and pulled out one of the benches to take a seat, quietly listening in on the exchange.

"Hello, this is Anne." A brief moment of silence followed as she listened to the person on the other end of the line. "You what? You're on your way here? Job? Ma'am, I have no idea what you're talking about. Who is this?"

Another moment of silence. As Morna walked into the kitchen through the entry at Callum's left, he raised a finger to shush her and pulled out the seat next to him.

"Who is she talking to?" Morna asked.

He shrugged and continued to watch Anne closely. She looked so flustered, and her eyes grew wider each second.

"Oh." Anne whispered the response and spun, wrapping the

cord around her as she faced them with a confused expression. "Well, yes, that is my email address. But I didn't...you know what, never mind. You're already on your way here. I'm sorry to hear about all of your delays. What's your next flight number?" She paused to listen, then said, "Don't worry about renting a car. We're kind of hard to find. I'll track your flight on my phone, and I'll make certain someone is there to pick you up in the morning."

Callum and Morna continued to stare with piqued curiosity as Anne stopped speaking for another brief moment. They sat up in attention when she spoke again.

"Uh-huh, okay, thanks for calling. See you tomorrow. Safe travels." As Anne hung up the phone, she pointed directly in Morna's direction. "You did this, didn't you?"

Callum stood and walked over to stand next to Anne in order to see Morna's face. He could tell by the irritated glint in Morna's eye that whatever this was, it had nothing to do with her.

"What exactly do ye think I did, dear?" the old woman asked.

Anne scowled. "Morna, come on. Are you really going to act like you didn't? That was a woman who says she received an email from me only a few days ago about the chef position here at the castle. Gillian and I opened the position up for applications seven months ago. A few weeks in, we received an excellent application. While I did type up an email asking the girl to come here for a test run, I never sent it because news of the fire reached me as I was typing the thing. It's been sitting in my draft folder for months. You must have sent it, right?"

"No, lass." Morna gave a harsh, humorless chuckle. "Even though yer cooking isna worthy of giving to a group of pigs, and it is taking everything in me to keep all of us from starving each night after yer efforts in the kitchen, I dinna do any such thing."

Callum hadn't been this entertained by anything in ages. He only hoped the women wouldn't start swinging fists at one another.

Thankfully, Anne gathered herself and kept things civil. "I see.

Well, you can deny it all you want, but I know how you are, Morna. The woman's on her way here, though she missed her first flight, apparently, and is stuck in Paris for the night. She'll be landing first thing in the morning. One of us is going to need to pick her up."

Morna stood, pushing herself away from the island. She walked over to Callum and pushed two fingers right into the center of his chest. "This was Grier's doing, and it's exactly what I warned ye about." She shifted to look at Anne. "Doona ye dare pick up that woman. And ye best talk this fool out of doing the same. We are all better off leaving the girl stranded at the airport where she'll likely give up and fly on back home. For all we know, she could be working with Grier."

Callum expected that nothing he could say would calm her, but he tried his best, anyway. "Morna, even if Grier played a hand in this, 'tis most likely the lass knows nothing of it. How often do people know of their role in yer meddling plans?"

Her fingers hit his chest harder this time, and he had to grit his teeth to keep from wincing. "Doona ye ever compare my meddling to that of Grier's, Callum."

"Who is Grier?"

Anne's question was well-meaning, but Callum would've done anything to prevent her asking it if he'd seen it coming.

"She is none of yer damn business, Anne." Morna turned and stomped out of the room, leaving Callum to deal with a weepy cook.

CHAPTER 7

"Blast ye, Grier. Blast ye for making me believe ye were dead and then using yer powers here without showing yer face. 'Tis time ye make yerself known. Whatever it is ye want with me or my family, get on with it, lest ye wish for me to start waging magic of my own. Would ye like to see which of us is more powerful? I wouldna think ye would, for we both know the answer."

Callum took one more step toward Morna, and he grimaced when she jumped in surprise. He'd made no effort to sneak up on her, but she was so wrapped up in her speech to the stairwell, he had frightened her.

"I'm sorry. I thought ye would see me," he said quickly. "What are ye doing out here, Morna? Ye were not kind to Anne. Ye need to go and apologize. Normally she doesna mind the teasing about her food, but ye are always so kind to her. It took her aback for ye to be so cruel. She had no part in this. She dinna deserve the way ye treated her."

She turned on him, anger in her eyes, and he readied for his own verbal beating. "Ye have no business telling me to apologize, Callum. Ye are not my father, ye are my friend."

Morna could lose her patience with him all she wished. He knew fear drove her strange and impatient behavior of late. "No, Morna. Ye doona get to behave this way. There is no reason for it. I doona understand what happened between this Grier and ye, but we've no proof that any of this has to do with her. Ye are frightened. I can see that, but ye have to stop this. Now."

He waited for her to unleash more anger on him. Instead, she wilted down onto the grass, shaking all over.

Gathering her up in his arms, Callum rubbed Morna's hands gently, pushing as much warmth as he could into her cold, trembling hands. He'd never seen the witch in such a state. He imagined few ever had.

"I've never been so frightened in my life, Callum. Nor have I ever been so out of control. If this is how most of ye live yer lives, I pity ye for it, for I doona care for it at all."

Sympathy for the old woman filled Callum. "I know that I doona have yer powers, Morna, but I dinna feel any evil near Grier when I saw her. I truly believe ye are worried for naught. Ye are making yerself ill over this. We've all enough to worry about, and we depend on ye too much for ye to be sick."

He held her as she wept. He'd done a lot of that lately—with Jane, with Anne, with the wee babe, and now, even Morna. He'd grown up in the rough company of his father and brothers. The newly realized knowledge that he was good at comforting women surprised him greatly.

"Aye, I know it," Morna sobbed. "Fear makes us all do foolish things, I suppose. I'll apologize to Anne at once. Ye dinna listen to me, did ye? About the lass? Someone will go and get her?"

Not a one of them, regardless of Morna's fears, was apt to leave the poor girl waiting at the airport. "Aye, Morna. She'll be coming to the castle. Though, I doona know where we will fit her in."

"Fine. Help me up. Please, just heed my warning. Be careful

with this girl, Callum. We doona know enough about her. I, for one, willna trust her until we do."

He hoped Morna's fears would abate soon. Everyone was used to her being so grounded, so open and loving to all. Suspicion didn't suit her.

"Fine," he assured her. "I will be wary of the woman until we all know her better. But let's give her a chance, aye?" She answered his plea with a glare, and he laughed as he dared to ask one more question. "I'm not comparing ye and Grier, but why do ye see yer interfering on the behalf of others differently than ye see Grier's?"

Morna pulled away from him, rolled herself to her knees, and pushed herself up from the ground. Staring down at him, she said, "I meddle for the sake of love, Callum. Grier meddles for her own amusement. I fear ye shall know the difference firsthand soon enough."

CHAPTER 8

Callum sat back in his seat at the long wooden table directly across from Morna, with the rest of the castle's temporary inhabitants gathered around. Morna rarely chatted this freely at the dinner table. While no one would ever call the witch quiet, Callum knew her to be the sort that very much enjoyed listening to others converse—especially her family.

Each evening when they gathered together for another of Anne's well-meaning but horrible meals, Morna would sit back, delighting in whatever new story the children had to tell about their imaginative adventures that day. She obviously relished every word about how work on the Cagair of his own time had gone that day.

But this evening was different. Rather than chiming in when the conversation called for her to do so, his friend led the conversation aimlessly, bouncing from topic to topic as if she couldn't settle her mind on just one thing. Callum couldn't stand it another moment. It was time to do as he'd promised her earlier. It was time that everyone learned of Cagair Castle's newest resident.

"Anne." He stood, drawing the attention of everyone at the table. "Might I speak with ye a moment?"

Callum ignored all of the confused expressions aimed at him and left for the kitchen to wait for Anne to join him. He would stay true to his word, but first he needed to make Anne understand the need for him to do so.

"What was that about?" she asked.

He leaned against the doorway, turning to face Anne as she paused midway down the steps leading to the kitchen. "Did Morna apologize to ye?"

"Yes, she did. I accepted. What's going on?"

"I've been torn between the two of ye lassies all day. Ye are both so stubborn that neither one of ye will work this out between yerselves. Ye are quite a pair. I shouldna be involved in this at all."

Anne rolled one of her hands dramatically in the air to hurry him on. "All right. We're a pain. I know. Get on with it."

"I know I told ye that I'd keep yer secret if ye thought it best to surprise everyone with the girl's arrival, but Morna has made me see differently. Everyone needs to know before she is picked up tomorrow."

Anne's face reddened in anger. "Is that why Jerry didn't come down for dinner? She doesn't want him to know about this Grier person? Morna has nothing to do with this. I'm hiring someone to work here. That's my job. Or at least it will be once the work is done on the castle and everyone has gone home. This is my deal —not hers. I see no reason why Morna should have any say in how I handle this. I don't know how or why the email was sent, but I'm glad it was. I'm so freaking sick of trying to cook for you guys that I would hire anyone that showed up wanting the job."

Callum allowed her to finish venting. He understood her frustration, but it would change nothing.

"Aye, ye are right about much of it, Anne. 'Tis yer job, and I doona think anyone will object to having the lass about, but ye know that 'tis not a normal situation here. There are things to decide. Things to talk over with everyone."

"Such as?"

"We must decide if we will tell her about the magic. Doona ye think it would be difficult to hide it from someone who not only works in the castle but lives here as well? The only reason this arrangement has worked so well during the castle's reconstruction is that everyone here knows the truth. Should we really feel comfortable introducing someone else to all of it? Such knowledge would change the lass's life forever."

He could sense by Anne's long, drawn-out breath that she could see the sense of such a discussion. It wasn't something to be decided lightly. Whatever the outcome, it would affect everyone at the castle.

"Okay, fine," she said. "I understand that, but that's not Morna's problem with the girl, is it? Morna has never had any problem introducing someone to magic. Every time we turn around, she's sending another girl across time to be wooed by one of you brutes."

He tried not to take offense to Anne's description of him and the other men of his time. He always thought himself a gentle sort of man on the inside. He expected the same was true of most of them. "Ye are right. 'Tis not the magic Morna is worried about. She believes this girl already knows of it, for Morna had no hand in sending yer email to the lass. I know she dinna respond well to ye before, but she's ready to tell all of ye about Grier and her suspicions now. And, aye, that is why Jerry is gone, though if he wakes before dinner is over and learns she put poppies in his drink, I fear a dreadful scene will unfold before our eyes. Still, the lass must be discussed with everyone whether ye like it or not."

He could see the resignation in Anne's eyes, and he didn't wait for her response. He stepped past her on the stairwell on his way back to the dining hall.

"Come, Anne. Let's not put this off any longer."

hen Callum and Anne returned, the children, save the babies, were gone from the table. Callum didn't know for certain what Morna would say, but the last thing she would want to do is frighten them. He expected she sent the children away to shield them from her words.

"All right, Callum. Now that ye've told Anne that she willna be surprising the lot of them tomorrow, I'm ready to speak with everyone."

"Please do," Jane said over the squeal of baby Nora in her arms. "I think the three of you have successfully put everyone's nerves on edge. Why did you send Cooper and the other little ones away?"

Callum walked around the table, offering to take the child from her so she could listen more closely. She handed the babe to him as soon as he approached. He smiled as the baby quieted the moment he gathered her in his arms. Whether it was the fire or their daily sessions with Morna for the months following, he didn't know, but he and the babe shared a special bond. It warmed Callum's heart to know she would always be able to call him uncle.

Morna gave him a quick questioning glance. As he nodded to encourage her, she said, "The time has come for me to tell ye more about me than I've ever had cause to before. Though, before I say a word, I'd like to preface it with this—doona ask me a single question. All of it brings back memories I doona wish to dwell on. I will tell ye what I must, and that will be all. Understood?"

Callum watched everyone nod in agreement as Morna paused briefly to prepare her words.

"We all know that magic exists at Cagair—the magic of another witch—a witch I long believed dead. She is not." Morna let that sink in for a moment, then continued, "It was she who put out the fire at Cagair, and it was she who saw fit to bring someone new into our midst now."

With Nora sleeping in his arms, Callum returned to his seat, allowing Morna to relay everything she had told him over the past days to the rest of the castle's residents. When she finished, a silence hung over the room in a way he'd not expected. He could sense the tension of many, their strong fear of a woman none of them knew.

He understood that Morna's past dealings with Grier made her fearful, but something deep within told him that perhaps, in this instance, his friend was wrong to be hasty with her judgment. He'd seen this Grier for himself—witnessed her power, sensed her presence. Even as he lay enveloped in the rising smoke, all he felt when he looked at her was her love for the burning castle. He knew in that moment, as his vision faded along with the flames that roared over his castle, that the witch had come to save his home out of her own real and desperate love for Cagair Castle.

Time had a way of distorting memories. What if time somehow veiled the truth about Grier from Morna? What if whatever happened between them blurred Morna's reality of past events after all this time?

Adwen's voice stirred him from his thoughts.

"Morna, ye are right. If this woman knows of the magic like ye think she does, then it means she works with this Grier, and she comes here with intent. We canna allow her to be here without knowing the extent of her knowledge about the castle's magic. When she arrives in the morning, we must question her, the lot of us. If we're all gathered, perhaps she will be frightened enough to tell us the truth. If she doesna do so, Morna can spell her so that she has no choice."

Callum stood, quickly looking over to his right where Blaire already held her hands extended toward him to accept the baby. When his hands were free, he slammed his fist down on the table. Adwen was always hasty with his decisions, but how could he possibly think it good to apprehend the lass and scare her to death when her innocence was far more likely than her guilt?

"Ye are a fool if ye think I will allow that for a moment." Callum turned his angry eyes away from his brother to address Morna. "I'm sorry, Morna, but yer suspicion is not enough for us to treat this lass any differently than we would anyone else."

Orick's voice, deep and booming, joined in from across the room. "Callum's right. I've not had the same experiences with Morna as the rest of ye have, so forgive me if my words cause offense. Have we not all learned by now that witches doona usually enlist the help of others in their meddling?"

Callum wanted to jump across the table and hug Orick in thanks for his wisdom. Not that it surprised him—Orick was always the sound and steady mind to Adwen's changing and reckless one.

Morna joined him by rising to her feet, demanding everyone's attention before a single person in the room could answer Orick's question. She pointed at Callum. "Ye can sit now. I'm taking charge of this conversation once again." Twirling to her right, she pointed at Orick. "Seeing as ye only know the one witch," she pointed to herself, "me, I think it best ye keep yer opinions about witches in general to yerself." Adwen was the last to get her angry finger pointed in his direction. "And, Adwen, Callum is right. What were ye thinking suggesting we all but take the lass captive? I'm frightened, but I saw fit to tell ye my fears so we could discuss them. I'm not cruel, nor am I a criminal. Jane's sure to give ye hell for that suggestion later."

Callum looked over at Jane to see her nodding her head in agreement. Her arms were crossed and her teeth clenched as she spoke. "Oh, you have no idea." Jane twisted her head to speak directly to her husband. "You can be so stupid sometimes."

Callum seated himself at Morna's request and leaned back to listen silently as he tried to keep from laughing at the wounded expression on Adwen's face.

"Now," said Morna more calmly. "I'll continue as I meant to before Adwen interrupted me and Callum and Orick saw fit to cast me as a crazy criminal. My first thought was that we needn't pick up the girl from the airport, but 'twas a foolish notion, for I'm sure she'll show up either way. I've had time to calm down. Here is what I suggest." Clearing her throat, she continued, "We must all be cautious with the lass, but I will not allow anyone to be unkind to this girl. I can see now that fear of Grier has turned me into a bit of a monster. I allow her to win if I continue on in such a way.

"Of course, we willna be apprehending our visitor as soon as she arrives, but we must find out if she knows of the magic. Who is going to pick the lass up tomorrow?"

Callum raised his hand. He and Anne had already agreed on the arrangement. "I am."

Morna nodded and reached into her pocket before rolling a small vial across the table toward him. "I should've known. O'course ye are. Ye will give her this. I doona care how ye get it down her throat, but ye must promise me that ye will. Doona worry, it willna hurt the lass at all. All it will do is make certain that she canna lie to us while she's here. That way, we will verra quickly learn if she knows of the magic.

"If she does, we will inquire further about what Grier has sent her here to do. If she does not, I suggest that we keep quiet on the subject for at least a week so we have time to see how she works out. If Gillian and Anne, seeing as the lass will be working for them in the near future, find her work pleasing and she fits in well, we will tell her everything then. I doona see how anyone can live here without learning of the magic. 'Twould be best that she knows everything if she stays here long-term. Does everyone agree, or do I need to keep speaking until ye all see sense and get on board with my plan?"

Callum twirled the glass vial in between his fingers. He didn't like the idea of tricking the stranger in any way, but he could see that Morna's thinking was more rational now than the last time he spoke with her. Her plan was a sensible one, and he expected everyone would agree.

"Aye, I'll give the lass this before I arrive here with her in the morning," he agreed. "Does everyone else agree to do as Morna suggested? We can broach the subject of magic with our visitor over dinner her first night here, if so."

It didn't take long for everyone to agree, and the matter was settled among them all.

Only when Callum stood to leave the table did he see Jerry standing outside the dining hall, out of sight but surely not out of earshot. Morna's poppies were not as strong as she'd hoped. Clearly, Jerry had been awake for some time. Tears ran down the old man's face, and Callum didn't dare approach him for fear of embarrassing his friend. Whatever reason Morna had for keeping word of Grier from Jerry, it mattered not.

Jerry now knew everything. Callum was sure of it.

CHAPTER 9

By the time I actually landed in Scotland, some twelve hours later than originally scheduled, I was exhausted, frustrated, and ready to collapse. All that kept me from stopping for a quick nap on an airport bench was the knowledge that I didn't have to drive myself to the castle.

So while I stood in baggage claim waiting for my bag to come around the carousel, I did my best to be grateful for small blessings. By the time I grabbed my bag, I felt better about everything and hurried outside to look for my escort.

When I first spotted him in the pick-up area, I started at the sight of him. I didn't know if they just didn't make men like him in Italy, or if he was truly as good looking as he seemed to me. It had been a long time since I'd stepped out of my sleepy village, but I found my escort to be immensely attractive.

He was tall, but not freakishly so. He wore a dark green sweater that hugged him just tightly enough so that anyone could tell that he didn't have an ounce of fat on his body. His tan corduroy pants, while not the most normal piece of clothing I'd ever seen, suited him.

I could tell he didn't have a clue what I looked like—not that he would have reason to—and I appreciated the moment of anonymity so I could stand back and really look him over.

His hair was thick and full, and I had the strangest desire to run my fingers through it. I found my reaction to him ridiculous, but I still stood there and gawked at him for another long minute or so. He was just a guy, most likely one with a completely average, dull personality. But while I studied him, I didn't care one bit how boring he would most likely turn out to be.

I was watching him lean against the car and cross his arms in such a way that his muscles bulged out against the sweater when the snicker of the middle-aged woman standing next to me shook me out of my teenage-like stupor. I reached down to grab my suitcase sitting on the ground next to me.

"Oh dearie, ye're in trouble with that one, I can tell ye right now," the woman said. "I suppose ye are the one he's waiting for then? Ye best close yer mouth and blink a few times so ye doona look so doe-eyed before ye walk over to him. Never let a man see how much ye like him."

"Right." I stood and straightened myself, smiling at the woman in thanks. "I don't even know him. He's just picking me up to take me to my new job. He's probably awful."

The stranger shook her head and laughed. "Lass, it wouldna matter two twats to me if he was the dullest man in the country. If I was fifteen years younger, I'd be racing ye over there."

We chuckled loudly together before I bid her goodbye. Her words had done me good—I felt much less foolish about gawking at the man after my brief conversation with her.

Grabbing my things, I walked toward him, determined to behave as the grown-up woman I was.

———

allum didn't see her until she spoke to him, her delicate hand sliding into view as he stared down at his feet, lost in his thoughts. When he looked up into her eyes, he nearly swallowed his tongue. Even when Morna said she feared Grier's hand in the woman's arrival, he'd not thought about the possibility that it would be the lass he'd seen so many months before.

"Hi. I'm Sydney."

It took him a moment, but he finally regained his composure. Callum only hoped the shock hadn't remained on his face too long as he took her hand. The feel of it made the muscles in his stomach clench. The blurry outlines he'd seen of her months ago did little justice to her beauty.

"Ye may call me Callum. Welcome to Scotland."

"Thank you. Do you want me to put these in the back?"

As she stepped away from him, her hair blew in the wind, and the fragrance from the strands nearly undid him. He moved quickly to step in front of her, reaching for her bags. "No, lass. Ye needn't do that. I'll put them in the back. Go ahead and get in. 'Tis a bit of a drive back to Cagair."

As he stowed her bags into the trunk, Callum realized he needed the moment away from her to heed Morna's warning. He grasped onto the vial, reminding himself of what he needed to do. It did seem likely that magic was involved since Sydney was the same woman he'd seen in his visions. Although, by the looks of her, she didn't appear to be one that meddled with witches or even knew of their true existence. Still, he would do his utmost to find out.

Closing the trunk, he walked to the driver's side and climbed in. Immediately, the small space between them seemed electric with tension. He placed the car in drive and pulled away from the airport, following the strange moving map Anne had strapped to his dash so he wouldn't get lost. He loved driving—it was the first skill he'd insisted on learning during his time in the twenty-first century.

Once he had his bearings, he said, "Have ye been to Scotland before?"

"No, this is my first time here."

Her voice was pleasant—smooth and kind—just as he had imagined it to be.

"Why would ye want a job here?"

"I just really needed a change. There was no time for life in my old job. It was day in, day out. I just couldn't do it anymore. It surprised me to receive a response from Cagair after so much time, though. I sent in the application, like, half a year ago."

"Aye. I'm sure 'twas surprising."

Surely that response alone was proof enough that she was as much a pawn in Grier's meddling as the rest of them. Her surprise sounded genuine to him.

"It was a good surprise, though," Sydney added. "A bit of a saving grace, really. It came at just the right time."

He couldn't do it. He couldn't give her the potion as Morna wished him to. Sydney knew nothing of magic. He knew it just as surely as he knew that Morna was liable to strangle him once she learned about his decision. He felt drawn to the lass, and he wanted her to trust him. How could she if he spelled her only minutes after they met?

"In regard to surprises, lass," he said, "I feel I should give ye a warning about what awaits ye when we arrive."

He could hear her move slightly in her seat, but he didn't dare glance over for fear the sight of her might distract him. The last thing he wanted to do was send the both of them flying off into a ditch.

"Oh?"

"Aye. Ye see, there was a mix-up with the email. 'Twas sent on accident."

"What? Do you already have a chef?" She huffed a

disappointed sigh. "Someone really should have told me that on the phone when I called. I wouldn't have come the rest of the way."

He hurried to reassure her, unthinkingly reaching out to squeeze her hand. She gasped at his touch. "No, lass. 'Tis not that. The opening of the castle has been delayed for some time. The owner is hosting family so she and the woman who helps in the castle's running delayed their search for a time. But a chef is needed, believe me."

"Oh, good. You scared me. I was about to be so embarrassed."

He could hear the relief in her voice. If he hadn't already decided against giving her the potion, he most certainly would have then.

He cleared his throat. "One other thing...there is an old woman staying at the castle. Her name is Morna. She's a good friend to all of us, but she's not all there anymore, if ye get my meaning. She often rambles on about things that doona make sense. If she says anything to ye or asks ye strange questions, doona worry yerself over it. Just be kind and answer truthfully, for she willna remember yer answers nor her questions come morning."

It was an awful but necessary lie.

CHAPTER 10

Once I actually met Callum, it was easy to be around him. Not that I found him less attractive once I got in the car with him—the exact opposite was true—but there was no reason for me to turn into the gawking, shaky fool I'd been for those few short moments at the airport. He was kind, smart, and had a sort of quiet funniness about him that was incredibly charming.

At one point during the drive to Cagair, he even reached over and gave my hand a gentle squeeze. While unexpected, I appreciated his soft, reassuring touch very much. When we pulled onto the narrow road leading to Cagair, I realized that I couldn't recall a single glimpse of scenery that we had passed by on our way, thanks to how much his conversation distracted me.

Luckily, when the job was officially mine, this would be my home. I'd have more than enough time to really explore everything properly.

"Here we are, lass. This is Cagair Castle. I doona think there is a prettier structure in all of Scotland."

I wasn't about to disagree. Even though I had no firsthand knowledge of the country, I couldn't imagine anything being more splendid. "It's beautiful."

"As are ye."

I knew I blushed at his words—my fair cheeks always did when I was embarrassed—but I managed to play his compliment off as if it were a casual statement. I was certain that was how he'd meant it, no matter how sweetly he said it.

I cocked my head at him, smiled, and pulled up one of my shoulders in a quick little nervous movement as I unbuckled my seatbelt. "Well, thanks. That's a very kind thing for you to say."

As he shut off the engine to the car, he jumped out to come around and open my door before running around the back to gather my luggage. "Go on in," he instructed. "I'm certain Anne is waiting for ye. I'll see these up to yer room."

I wondered then, as I nervously approached the stairs leading up to the castle's main doors, just what exactly Callum's role was here at the castle. Was Anne his wife? Did he simply work here? Our talk of my old job and his warning about the castle had left me little time to ask him.

"Hello, Sydney. I'm happy you made it safely. Aren't delays just the worst?"

I looked up at the voice to see a woman around my own age waving me to the top of the stairs. She smiled at me as I approached.

"You must be Anne. I'm very pleased to meet you. Yes, delays are awful. I hoped to arrive with much more energy than I have now."

She shook her head sympathetically, placing a hand on my shoulder as she ushered me to the side of the doorway. "I can't even imagine. Now, before I bring you inside, I better let you in on what's going on here since you're about to be inundated with nosy people. If I know Callum, he's already told you that we weren't really expecting you; however, I am thrilled you're here. We are filled to the brim with people right now—not guests but close friends and family. They're all busy working, but you'll meet them at dinner this evening. We'd love for you to join us so you can get to know everyone."

"I'm up for whatever you need me to do. You're the boss." I looked over my shoulder to see Callum approaching with my bags. I hoped that I'd not been too presumptuous by not securing lodging elsewhere. However, judging by the location of the castle, I doubted there was anywhere else for me to stay. "I know I'm not actually hired yet, but I did bring my things. Do you have room for me? If not, I'm sure I can figure something out. How far is the nearest town?"

"Oh, you're hired. Everyone has lost weight since I took over the cooking, and only a few of us had any weight to lose to begin with. Callum will set up your room for you and will leave your things there. Then he's got to scurry along and get to his own work."

Callum gave me a quick nod and a smile before entering in the main doors ahead of us. I started to ask him what his job was, but before I could say another word, Anne whisked me inside and opposite the direction Callum had gone. She moved so quickly I had little time to take in the castle's interior before we reached the top of a set of stairs that Anne informed me led down to the kitchen.

"Come on down. The kitchen is in the basement. It's where it originally would have been. Gillian really did her best to restore everything exactly right. It's all modernized, but we didn't change its location."

I didn't know who Gillian was, but I expected to get answers to all of my questions soon enough.

I followed her down the steps and into the prettiest kitchen I'd ever seen. They had done more than modernize it—they made it a topnotch workspace worthy of even the pickiest of chefs. It put the kitchen in my restaurant to shame, boasting a total of twelve gas burners, six separate ovens, two large dishwashers, two refrigerators, one large freezer, a wide assortment of first class copper pots and pans hanging above a grand workspace of an island. I was certain my mouth gaped open in astonishment. I stood there awkwardly as I struggled to form a response that matched my awe of the place.

"Wow, Anne. This is amazing."

Anne laughed and pulled out one of the island's barstools for me.

"I'm glad you think so. It is nice, but I hate it with every fiber of my being. I am so glad you're here to take over. I've cooked for everyone most nights for the last six months, and not a single meal has turned out well. The most common reviews given to me by my friends are bland, burnt, and badly done."

I couldn't resist a small laugh as she plopped down dramatically next to me. I imagined she was going to be a lot of fun to work for. At least she had a sense of humor.

"Oh, you can't be that bad," I said.

Anne stood, marched over toward one of the refrigerators, and pulled something out before setting it in front of me. "Have you eaten breakfast? I saved you a plate so you could see what I mean. Give me a minute to heat it up."

I waited patiently. When she finally slid me a plate of seasoned potatoes, sliced sausage, and what looked like a spinach and cheese quiche, I suspected she'd grossly over-exaggerated her inabilities. Everything looked like it would taste great. As I lifted the first forkful into my mouth, I expected to taste something that was, at its worst, only decent.

I was dreadfully wrong.

I'd not tasted such terrible cuisine in a very long time. I tried to chew the mouthful politely, but by the second clench of my jaw, I couldn't choke it down. Politely spitting it into my napkin, I stood and carried my plate over to the trash can, sliding the contents inside before I turned to comfort the crestfallen Anne.

"Well, that's all right. You just haven't acquired a knack for it yet. Why don't I give you a quick lesson? You can help me get familiarized with the kitchen in the process."

Anne smiled and reached over to a set of hooks on the wall to grab us each an apron. "Sounds perfect. Teach me to cook one dish perfectly. Then, I'm turning it all over to you. By dinner, the kitchen will be officially yours."

CHAPTER 11

My mother was a nervous woman, no matter the situation. She was just as nervous making her weekly trips to the grocery store as she would be meeting the Queen of England. She could make herself sick with worry over just about anything. Mom was stunning and looked wonderful in everything she wore, but there were always at least half a dozen outfit changes before she ever left the house.

I was the exact opposite. Nothing rattled me. I could make myself at home in just about any situation, and my natural confidence was so at odds with her personality that she would always joke that she must have brought the wrong baby home from the hospital.

I didn't care what people thought about me. I knew what I thought about myself, and that was all that concerned me. If someone didn't like me—well—they were a fool.

My younger sister worried much like my mother. I always thought the nerves just skipped me, but today I felt more like the both of them than I ever had before. Never had the thought of picking out an outfit caused me such anxiety. Wrapped tightly in my favorite robe, I stared down at not six, not seven, but eight different outfits, and not a one of them seemed good enough. What did one wear to dinner in a castle? I didn't expect it to be formal, but how casual was too casual? I hadn't a clue.

Eventually, I decided on a pair of skinny jeans that I could tuck into a pair of black boots that went nearly up to my knee. I paired them with a dressy red sweater and called it good.

"Knock, knock."

I glanced up from my efforts to put away all of the clothes I'd tossed around so carelessly to see that I'd unintentionally left my door open slightly. Before I could answer, it slowly swung open the rest of the way as an ornate cart entered the room. Stepping toward the doorway, I looked to see who was pushing it—a bright-eyed little boy with the friendliest smile and cutest freckles ever.

"Well, hello there. You look a little young to be working. I sure hope this isn't your job." I smiled at him.

The young boy didn't miss a beat, laughing as he pushed the cart over to me, then pouring me a cup of coffee. "Nah, I don't work here. I'm just staying here with my family. I just wanted to come and say hi to you. You'll be seeing a lot of me, I'm sure. I like to run all over the place. I thought you might be tired, too, since you traveled so far. Do you want some coffee? I'm sort of like the official coffee maker around here."

I grinned and nodded at him, moving to sit at a small table near where he'd stopped his cart. "Yes, please. I am tired. I took a little nap earlier, but it didn't seem to do me a lot of good. I'm sure your coffee will help me immensely. May I ask your name? I'm Sydney."

He handled the coffee pot and little basin of creamer so carefully, stirring it all together before dropping two cubes of sugar into the cup. He didn't ask me how I liked it. I could tell from the precision of his pour and the familiarity of his movements that he probably made it the same way for everyone.

"Oh, coffee will help," he assured me. "Especially this cup—

Morna found the creamer. Usually, I just use the plain white stuff, but this one is supposed to taste like hazelnuts, I think. Hope that's okay."

"I'm sure it will be perfect."

He extended the cup to me. "Oh, I forgot. I'm Cooper."

"It's nice to meet you, Cooper. This is really so thoughtful. Thank you."

I lifted the drink to my lips, and I could see by the nervous jitter of his feet that he was waiting to see what I thought. I expected it to be sweet with as much sugar and creamer as he had placed in it, but instead a taste so bitter hit my tongue that I had to swallow hard to keep from spewing it all over him. Twice in one day I'd been assaulted by really terrible food and beverage. No wonder they were so desperate for a chef.

Doing my best to mask my disgust, I tried to smile, but my lips trembled a little as I opened them. I couldn't believe the words that came out of my mouth. "That is the worst coffee I've ever tasted." What was the matter with me? I knew better than to hurt a little boy's feelings. They hadn't at all been the words I'd meant to say. I braced myself to comfort what I expected to be a crying child.

The boy pulled his brows together and crossed his arms inquisitively. "Terrible? That's not possible, ma'am. I make really good coffee. Everybody says so. Unless..." he paused and pointed at the tray. "It wasn't my coffee but the creamer. I'll find out for you. Don't drink another sip."

His lack of distress surprised me. But there wasn't any chance of me taking another sip. While I didn't really want him to have to taste the atrocity of his concoction, I could see I wouldn't be able to stop him.

Cooper started by pouring just a little bit of straight coffee into a separate cup, taking a quick swig and swishing it around in his mouth. His face gave nothing away. "Nope. Not my coffee," he said. He then reached for a cube of sugar, swiftly popping it into his mouth. He smiled while it dissolved. "Definitely not the sugar. Only one thing left."

I grimaced as he brought the basin of creamer to his lips and threw back a swallow big enough to kill a horse.

Gagging, the boy fell back onto his bottom as he spit and made a horrible face in between disgusted groans. "Oh my gosh. Do you think it's spoiled?"

Remembering an unopened bottle of water in my bag, I ran over to grab it for him, tossing it in his direction. "It doesn't taste spoiled. It just tastes awful. You should probably tell your friend not to give it to anyone else. Are you all right?"

Cooper stood, shook himself off, and gulped the water from the bottle. "Yeah, I'm fine. I'm gonna have to let Morna have it, though. She had to have known that didn't taste good. I'm so sorry. How about some coffee with just plain sugar?"

I couldn't possibly stomach another sip of coffee, but the woman's name the boy mentioned rang a bell it hadn't before. "Oh, no thank you. I'm fine. I think that sip woke me right up. Did you say Morna helped you with this?"

"Yeah."

"Callum warned me about her, I think. She's kind of crazy, right?"

The boy snickered and walked over to sit in the chair opposite me. "Ha. She wouldn't like it if she knew Callum said that. She's a little different, but it's not because she's crazy. It's because she's a witch."

"A witch?" Curious. I crossed my arms and leaned back in my chair. I knew children often made up stories, but Cooper didn't seem the type. His comment had been so nonchalant that I didn't have the slightest idea how to respond to him.

Nodding, he answered, "Yeah, she's a real good one, too. My stepdad got sliced right down the middle with a sword, so my step-uncle and my step-aunt sent him forward in time to stay at

Morna's place. She healed him. She didn't do it with medicine. She did it with magic."

"He went forward in time?" I gasped and raised my voice so that I would sound interested rather than confused. Clearly, he was indulging me in some sort of fairy tale, but the lack of lead up to the story caught me off guard.

"Yeah, but we go back in time and then forward again all the time around here. I actually live in the year sixteen forty-nine, but I was born in New York City in the year two thousand and eight."

I did some quick math in my head. The young boy was six, or nearly seven, with an imagination to rival just about anyone, I was sure. "Well, that is just amazing. What has you staying at the castle now?"

"Oh, well that's a bit of a long story."

I couldn't wait to hear what he came up with. Giving my watch a quick glance, I nodded and settled in for a tale. "I've got time. Tell me everything."

***

Callum hoped Sydney would be back in the kitchen by now. He didn't want to enter his bedchamber to retrieve his shoes while she was in there. If he did, she would know he'd moved out just to give her a bedroom, and he knew she wouldn't want that. The tower would suit him just fine, though. Anne had a comfy cot placed near the heater, and he could always run over to Orick's when he needed a shower.

He heard the sound of voices as he approached the door, and nearly turned away to come back at a later time. But when he heard the words being said, he stopped short outside the doorway.

"Let me get this straight. Almost everyone living at the castle now actually lives back in time, and each morning they travel down an outside staircase and into the past?"

It was Sydney's voice. Who was she with? Who would be so foolish as to tell her about the magic outright? More than that, why did Sydney not sound horrified by the revelation? Was it possible that he'd been wrong about her, and she really had known all along?

Callum took a step closer to listen in further.

"Yep. That's right."

Cooper's voice. The boy hadn't been present when everyone had agreed upon their plans regarding Sydney, but his mother told Callum that she'd spoken with Cooper about keeping quiet in regards to the magic. Why would he disobey?

"Wow. And this staircase...do you think you have time to show it to me before supper?" Sydney asked.

Callum couldn't wait any longer. He needed to intervene now before Cooper saw fit to drag the lass back into his own time. He stepped into the room, announcing his presence with a reprimand he directed at Cooper. "Lad, did yer mother not speak with ye about how we were to interact with our guest?"

Before Cooper had time to respond, Sydney approached him and laid a hand on his shoulder. A jolt of something like electricity shot through him at her touch.

"He's fine," she assured him. "Cooper hasn't bothered me at all, I promise. Somebody should really get this little fellow a notepad and some paper because he could be a writer. I've never seen a kid with such a vivid imagination."

Callum audibly sighed in relief at the realization that she didn't believe a word of Cooper's stories. "Aye, he does that." He glared at Cooper in an effort to keep him from saying more, but it was too late. The lad was already on his feet and ready to defend himself.

"Imagination? I wasn't making any of that up, Callum, and you know it. Tell her. I don't want her to think I was just lying to her."

Callum pulled away from Sydney and moved to crouch down beside Cooper. He whispered his words to the boy, hoping Sydney stood far enough away not to hear. "Cooper, what are ye doing? Dinna ye give yer mother yer word that ye wouldna do this?"

The boy's eyes grew wide with regret as he answered. "Yeah, I did promise her. I know I did. I don't know what's wrong with me. Every time she asks me a question, I can't say anything but the absolute truth. I try. I think of what I'm going to say, but instead something else comes out. Do you think Sydney is a witch, Callum?"

Callum looked back over his shoulder to see that Sydney had politely stepped away from them. "She's not a witch, Cooper. What are ye doing in here anyway?"

"It was Morna's idea. Mom told me I should wait until supper to meet her, but then Morna suggested that she might be kind of sleepy, and I should make her some coffee. So I did."

The potion. Understanding hit him immediately. Somehow, Morna knew he'd not given it to Sydney. He spotted the tray holding Cooper's coffee and noticed the basin of cream right away.

"Cooper, ye never serve coffee with cream. Morna gave it to ye, aye?"

The boy nodded. His furrowed brow told Callum how confused he was.

"And ye tasted this cream, aye?"

"Yeah, but only after Sydney tried it and told me that it was the worst coffee she'd ever tasted. I had to make sure it wasn't actually my coffee that tasted bad because we all know that's not possible."

"O'course. Ye are the master of coffee, lad. Doona worry. I'm not mad at ye. 'Tis Morna's fault, not yers. She spelled the cream. Ye canna lie. Neither can Sydney, I imagine. Have ye asked her anything since she drank this?"

Cooper shook his head and leaned in closer to whisper to him. "No. She wouldn't stop asking me stuff. It's exhausting telling that much truth."

Callum chuckled and moved to usher the boy from the room. "Aye, go and take a rest then. I'll clear all of this up with Morna. See ye at supper."

Once Cooper was gone, Callum turned to face Sydney. She didn't look pleased with him at all.

"I think you hurt his feelings," she said. "You really didn't need to scold him, Callum. I enjoyed his company. He was just telling stories. Isn't that what children do?"

"Not stories like that, lass. Doona worry, he's fine. He served ye some bad coffee, aye?"

He watched as her face distorted at the mere mention of it. "Oh my gosh, it was the worst thing I've ever tasted. And you know what? I actually said that to him. What's the matter with me? What happened in my mind at that moment that made me think it was okay to insult a little boy's efforts like that?"

"Nothing is wrong with ye, lass. Though I'm afraid ye will have many instances this night where ye are surprised at the things ye say."

She stepped toward him, and he moved from her path so she could pass him. She bobbed her head toward the door so he would follow her as she walked. "I need to go back down to the kitchen. You're welcome to come along if you'd like. I could use some help hauling some of the food upstairs." She hesitated a few moments before adding, "What did you mean by that? Why would I be surprised by anything that comes out of my own mouth?"

There was no need for him to explain. It wouldn't be long before she knew exactly what he'd meant. "Come dinner, ye will understand, and I couldna be more sorry for it," Callum told her.

CHAPTER 12

"Are ye pleased with yerself, Morna? Are ye happy that ye've gone and spelled young Cooper?"

Morna already knew what had happened with the potion. Otherwise, Callum knew she wouldn't be waiting for him in the tower. Her eyes looked as guilty as he'd ever seen them.

"No, I am not happy. I'm not happy about the mix-up, and I'm not happy that I had to be the one to give her the potion. If ye'd done what ye said ye would, none of this would've happened. Why dinna ye give it to her this morning, Callum?"

How could she possibly have known? He still held the vial inside his shoe. "I dinna give it to her because there was no reason to do so. She knew nothing of the magic until Cooper told her."

"And..." Morna leaned forward as if expecting him to continue.

"And what?"

"Did she seem surprised at his mention of the magic?"

"She dinna believe him. She thought he was telling her a tale."

Morna scoffed and threw her head back dramatically. "Ha. Or she was just pretending that she dinna believe him."

"Morna, Sydney had already sipped of yer potion. She couldna have lied about it."

Morna glanced awkwardly down at her feet in embarrassment, but she recovered from her mistake quickly. "Oh, well. We shall find out soon enough if she truly is naïve of the magic. I willna believe it until I ask her myself. I am sorry that Cooper fell victim to the potion and that he said anything about the magic to her, but there is little I can do about it now."

Callum was sorry for it as well. Sydney now knew the truth, even if she didn't believe it. They would have to tell her, to show her everything much earlier than any of them had planned to.

"Morna, we should not wait a week to tell Sydney about the portal. The lass quit her job. She has no plans to leave here. Regardless of what she believed at the time, she's already been told everything. It will not take long for her to see things that would make her suspect. We must tell her tonight."

Morna nodded and extended another small vial in his direction.

"No. Doona give me another one of yer mixtures," he said, waving it away. "I want nothing to do with them."

"Callum, take the blasted vial. The lass may verra well want what's inside by the end of this evening."

He frowned and moved to sit on the cot, realizing as he bent to remove his working shoes that he'd forgotten to get his other pair from his prior room. "I doubt that verra much, Morna."

"I intend to ask the girl some questions over dinner. She will find them odd, but she will answer them truthfully. Then we will tell her the truth. If history is any indication, I know just how it will go. She will think us all mad until she sees the proof with her own eyes.

"She will need to be taken down the stairwell, Callum. 'Tis the only way she will believe it. It should be ye that takes her back, not only because of yer connection to Cagair but because I can tell ye fancy her. Ye have a way about ye, Callum, that women find calming. Ye have even managed to calm me down on occasion. That's an accomplishment not many can claim. She will take it better from ye than she will from any other; I'm sure of it.

"When she believes it, if she wishes she dinna know, if it troubles or frightens her, then that is what this vial is for. If she takes it before bed, she will wake remembering nothing of the magic, and we can go on trying to hide it from her for as long as we can. Mayhap with time, when she's not so new to this castle and to us, she will accept the knowledge more readily."

Morna paused and moved to sit next to him.

Callum took the vial she slipped into his hands.

"She's the one ye saw, is she not?" Morna asked. "The one ye thought a ghost?"

"Aye. She is."

Morna nodded. "Then ye must understand that whether she knows about Grier or not, Grier brought her here. Just be wary is all. I love ye, Callum. I think of ye as the son I never had. Tell me ye will be careful with the lass."

"I will."

Unlike Cooper and Sydney, no truth potion had passed his lips. The words slipped out easily. Even though he wanted to mean them, he knew he did not. The lass didn't need magic to wield power over him. He was quite under her spell already.

* * *

"Chicken's done. Vegetables are roasted. Bottles of wine are open and ready for pouring. Breadbasket is warm. Table's set. Dessert will be ready by the time everyone is finished with dinner."

I stood in front of the shiny stove vent checking out my reflection, looking for any stray hairs or pieces of food on my face while I talked aloud to myself, running through my mental list to make certain everything was completed and ready for dinner.

I had overcooked; I was certain of it. Even if the number of guests exceeded sixty people, there would be more than enough food. But after all of the talk from Callum, Cooper, and Anne—the only inhabitants of the castle I'd met so far—everyone was near starving at the hands of Anne's cooking, so I wanted to make sure there was enough food for everyone to eat as much as they wished.

I couldn't help but wonder why no one else took over the job of chef before I arrived if they all thought Anne's cooking was so terrible. On second thought, I could tell she was the sort to never give up on anything. Chances were, she wouldn't allow anyone else to take over even if they'd wanted to. I imagined the only reason she was letting me was because I was a trained professional, not one of her friends or family members who'd constantly given her a hard time about her skills.

"It smells like heaven in here, lass. I could smell it all the way in my room."

I jumped at the sound of the voice and turned to see an old, frail-looking man walking down the steps and into the kitchen. His knees cracked loudly with each step, but it didn't seem to bother him in the slightest. He never paused or slowed his pace at all. From his stature, I guessed he'd never been all that tall, but I could see there was certainly a time in his life where he'd been taller than he was now. Time had curved his shoulders into a deep hunch, and I thought he looked much harsher than his voice sounded.

When he reached the bottom of the steps, he smiled at me, walking toward me with arms wide open for a hug. I happily met him halfway, delighted to be greeted so warmly. It made me feel at home with him immediately.

"I'm Jerry. Ye must be Sydney, our savior. I canna say enough bad things about the slop we've been eating as of late." He released me and moved to sit on one of the stools at the island.

I followed and sat down next to him. "That seems to be the

general consensus," I said with a laugh. "Poor Anne. What she made me this morning looked beautiful, but looks can be deceiving."

Jerry chuckled and spun his stool so that he faced me. "That it can. Are ye married, lass? Or do ye have someone that ye love?"

Startled by the frankness of his questions, I grinned and winked at him, teasing him with my answer. "Are you asking me out, Jerry?"

"Ha." The old man chuckled for a moment then reached over to give my hand a tight squeeze. "No, lass. Ye are too pretty to be seen with the likes of me, though this day I'd gladly trade ye for my current wife if ye were only a half century older. I only ask because I wonder if ye know what it is like to love someone completely all while being so angry with them that ye doona wish to see or speak to them for a month. The juxtaposition of my emotions has me feeling ill all over. Do ye know what I mean?"

"Not personally, no, but I think it's a common malady of being married. I believe I've heard both my parents say something similar before."

"Well, then ye'll understand that I'm so angry with my wife that I doona think I can sit through dinner with everyone pretending that nothing is wrong when there verra much is."

I pushed myself away from the island and immediately set about preparing him his own very special plate.

"I certainly do understand. It is my opinion that it is best to be genuine in all things. If you don't want to be there, then there's no need for you to show up and pretend that you do."

"I knew I would like ye, lass." Jerry reached out and took the plate from my hands.

"Wait just a second. Let me pour you a glass of wine and a glass of water. I'll follow up behind you so you're not trying to balance everything with two hands."

He nodded and waited patiently for me at the bottom of the stairs. It wasn't until we reached another long corridor of rooms on the opposite side of the castle from my own room that Jerry spoke again. "Thank ye for this." Pausing, he opened the door next to us, stepping inside and placing his plate down before turning to collect the glasses I held out for him. "Sydney, do ye know anyone by the name of Grier?"

I shook my head, confused. "No. Does she live here? I haven't met very many people at the castle yet. I think my big introduction is meant to happen over dinner."

He smiled, and I thought I saw something resembling relief, or maybe confirmation, wash over his face. The wrinkles in his brow lessened a little, and his smile seemed a little brighter as he leaned in to kiss my cheek. "No, she doesna live here. I just had to ask ye. My wife's a fool. Ye doona need magic to trust the words of another."

He started to close the door, but I reached out to stop him. His statement only confused me further. "Magic? What do you mean?"

"Nothing. I doona wish to have anything to do with it, but Sydney, please know that I am sorry if dinner doesna go well for ye. Fear makes fools of those who let it take root."

He shut the door in my face before I could inquire further.

Why did every new conversation in this castle seem stranger than the last?

CHAPTER 13

When I returned to the kitchen, I heard the sound of footsteps above me. Right on time, everyone began to file into the dining hall for dinner. I didn't know the proper way to proceed with the meal. There were no waiters or waitresses, and there was no possible way I could carry all of the food up on my own. It also seemed quite rude to ask anyone to help me carry everything upstairs.

Thank goodness, I didn't have to ponder over the problem for very long. Just as I slipped on oven mitts and prepared to carry up two of the chickens, Anne, Callum, and a man I'd yet to meet appeared in the entryway. While I'd suggested earlier that Callum help me carry things upstairs, he hadn't seemed to hear me, instead disappearing quickly following his strange last words to me. I was happy to see him here now. Obviously, he hadn't completely ignored me before.

Anne quickly came over to join me. "Is everything ready to go?"

"Yes," I told her.

"It smells even better than it looks. That will be quite a change for everyone. If you're ready, we are here to help you carry everything up. I did suggest we install an elevator down here so we could bring carts up and down easily during mealtime, but my husband and the actual owner, Gillian, wouldn't have it. Apparently, an elevator crossed the line in terms of modernizing the place." Anne shrugged her shoulders apologetically. Slipping on a pair of oven mitts, she grabbed another chicken from the island.

The man I'd yet to meet approached next, forgoing a handshake and just nodding his head in greeting. I knew right away that he had to be the husband Anne referred to, and the relief I felt at learning it wasn't Callum surprised me immensely.

"Hello. I'm Aiden, Anne's husband and the one responsible for the lack of an elevator. My apologies. I'd shake yer hand, but ye've got them a little full. We're glad to have ye here. I canna tell ye how much."

He quickly grabbed a pair of mitts and reached for the large pan of roasted vegetables. I set my own chicken back down on the island as they left, giving everything a quick glance to see what would be best to have Callum carry.

"What's left?" he asked. "I've long arms, and I'm quite good at balancing things. Let's try to get the rest of it in one load, aye?"

I couldn't really imagine Callum being that graceful—one of his legs pulled awkwardly when he walked, giving him a sort of pained limp that I could tell he always did his best to hide.

I waited a brief moment until Aiden and Anne were far enough away that they wouldn't hear me question him. I'd been unable to stop thinking about his strange last words to me, and Jerry's warning on top of that left me determined to get to the bottom of whatever was going on. Why would Callum believe I would say many surprising things during dinner? What reason would I have to not know my own words before I said them? I wasn't a heavy drinker, and I actually did try to think about things before I spoke.

"You shouldn't need to balance anything. I already have wine and water on the table upstairs, and if you'll just stack the five breadbaskets up and carry those, I think I can manage the two remaining chickens. Do you think I cooked too much?"

He laughed, and my stomach fluttered at the sight of the deep dimple in his right cheek. I'd not seen it before, but when he smiled wide, it revealed itself clearly. I found it ridiculously attractive.

"Ye've not seen most of us yet, have ye?" Callum asked. "Ye wouldna ask that question if ye had. The men among us run large, and there are a few women—while tiny in size and stature—that can nearly out-eat us."

"No, the only people I've met are you, Anne, Cooper, Jerry, and now Aiden."

He took a step toward the stairs.

I moved in his path to stop him. "Wait. Don't go upstairs yet. What did you mean earlier?"

I could see in his eyes that he knew exactly what I referred to. I could also tell by the slight twitch of his bottom lip that he was going to lie. "I doona know what ye mean," he said. "There are people waiting upstairs. Everyone is anxious to meet ye. We should be on our way. Ye can sit next to me, and I'll tell ye who everyone is as the meal begins."

I shook my head, grounding my feet. Unless he intended to douse me with wine until my lips were so loose that I just started spouting out whatever thoughts popped into my head, his words before made no sense. "Nope. You know what I'm talking about. You almost said something different. Why would I be surprised by anything that came out of my own mouth? The only reason I was foolish enough to hurt Cooper's feelings before was because that coffee was so bad it shocked me into being stupid. It doesn't make sense to me at all. I've been thinking about it all day."

He waited a long moment. I couldn't tell if he was trying to make up a believable lie, or if he just hoped that I would give up and get out of his way. The latter was never going to happen.

"Sydney, I promise that ye doona wish for me to show ye what I meant. Let's just join the others."

"Show me? What does that mean? You have to show me now, because I am not moving. I will stand here all day and let the food grow cold and let everyone wonder where we are if you don't tell me now."

He chuckled and crossed his arms smugly, leaning against the counter as he stared back at me with amused eyes. "Fine. What do ye think of the castle?"

I frowned and shook my head at him, confused. I couldn't see what that had to do with anything. "What?"

"Just answer the question."

"I think it's amazing. I've lived in Italy for the last three years. They have some of the prettiest buildings in the whole world, and I don't think any of them are as beautiful as this. Satisfied?"

"No, lass. I'm only getting started. When ye first saw me this morning...what did ye think?"

"All I could think was *holy crap, he's the most gorgeous man I've ever seen.* I could scarcely breathe looking at you."

The moment after the words exited my mouth, I gasped. I always thought of myself as the sort of person who thought before I spoke, but what I'd just said had escaped me before I'd had the chance to make up a lie. The proper response would've been, "*I thought you were professional and kind, and I appreciated your warning.*" All of that was true, too, but it hadn't been my first thought. My first thought was what I'd spoken aloud—an admission so embarrassing that I feared I would never recover.

I nearly fell back into the refrigerator. I shook all over from shock, fear, and humiliation, but Callum just stood there grinning like the Cheshire Cat.

"What just happened?" I choked out. "How did you make me do that?" I would've crawled all the way inside the refrigerator if I could've.

Callum took one long step toward me. "I dinna do anything,

lass. Ye are the one that said the words. Ye wished to know what I meant, and I'm showing ye. What is yer greatest fear?"

I wanted to say something meaningless, like 'spiders and heights'. Instead, I said, "Ending up like my grandmother."

He took one more step, and I flattened myself against the cool stainless steel surface behind me. I didn't care that the handle buried itself in my back. His proximity made me nervous. His power over my words frightened me.

"Are ye angry with me, Sydney? I'm only doing what ye asked."

"No." I wasn't angry. Only confused.

"Good, I doona want ye to be angry with me." He took another step closer, leaving only inches between us. "Would ye be angry if I kissed ye, lass?"

"No." I whispered my answer this time, my heart pounding so hard inside my chest that I could hear the sound of it in my ears. I didn't want to say anything other than the truth. My legs were weak. My hands were trembling, and all I wanted was for him to gather me up in his arms. "No," I whispered again.

He leaned so that his mouth brushed up against my ear, which only made me shake harder. "Do ye want me to?" he asked.

My answer was breathless, needy. "Yes."

I could feel him smile against my ear, but instead of moving his lips to my own, he gripped my arms and stepped away, turning quickly to gather the baskets of bread on the island into his arms.

I stared after him, and my mood changed quickly. "Well, now I'm angry. I still haven't a clue how you did that. I'm rather frightened, and you're going to go through all of that and then not even kiss me?"

"Aye, lass, precisely. I willna be kissing ye now. Though it pleases me to know that ye'd like me to. Get yer chickens and follow me upstairs. Ye have lots of people to meet and so much more to learn. Doona worry, though. After all that I just asked ye, I suppose the rest of the evening willna be so difficult."

He took the stairs two at a time. I knew he did so to escape before I could question him further. It took me three more minutes to breathe deeply enough that my legs quit shaking.

He sure knew how to ruin a moment. Now I wanted to punch him in the nose more than I wanted to kiss him. I hoped he would give me the opportunity.

CHAPTER 14

Callum's entire body was tense. Never had it been so difficult for him to walk away from a woman, but he didn't want to kiss Sydney when her decision to tell him her desires wasn't her own. His questions were disrespectful enough. He wouldn't take further advantage of her spelled state by kissing her.

Still, it thrilled him to know that she was attracted to him in the same way he was to her. He would have to apologize to Morna—he was no longer as angry with her as he had been. Perhaps there were some benefits of hearing words that were most assuredly the truth.

When he entered the dining hall, everyone sat quietly at the table waiting for Sydney's arrival. Only Anne was standing. "Where is Sydney?" she asked. "Does she need more help?"

"No, Anne. She's fine. She'll be along shortly."

"Callum, why are your cheeks all red?" Cooper blurted. "Are you hot? If so, that's weird, because I'm freezing in here."

"Aye. I'm rather warm. Always am." Callum pulled out his chair and sat in his usual place next to Cooper, leaving the seat on his other side empty for Sydney. He found the castle's halls chilly, as well, but he wasn't about to tell Cooper the real cause of his reddened skin.

Anne spoke up, ignoring him as she headed toward the kitchen. "I think I'm going to go help her anyway. It's probably a lot for her to walk into this group unaccompanied. I'll be right back with her. Don't start talking to her all at once when she gets up here."

"Ah!" I screamed as I saw Anne bounding down the steps in my direction. With a roasting pan balancing on each arm, I knew if she didn't look up, we would likely collide at any moment. "Anne, stop."

She halted immediately. "Oh geez, that was almost a disaster, wasn't it? Let me take one of these birds for you. When we get upstairs, I'll introduce you to everyone. There's a whole bunch of us, so don't be too concerned about remembering everyone's name. It will take you a while."

I nodded, passing one of the chickens off to her and ignoring her suggestion completely. I wanted to remember every name and face, and I was certain I could. It was sort of my thing. I made a huge effort to pay close attention to everyone I met at first greeting.

Everyone fell silent the moment we entered. I pulled my shoulders back and walked as confidently as possible behind Anne.

"Okay guys," Anne announced, "I'm not going to make this real formal since we're among friends. Everyone say hello to Sydney. She's going to be the new chef around here, which means I'm going into leisure mode for at least the next few weeks in celebration of not having to cook for you ungrateful fools anymore."

Laughter trickled out around the table.

"Sydney comes to us from Italy," Anne continued. "She attended one of the best culinary schools in the world and has spent the last three years running a very popular restaurant in Tuscany."

Anne turned to me, and I knew she expected me to say a little something. "Hello, everyone. I just wanted to let you all know that I really am so happy to be here. And while Anne's introduction was lovely, please don't let my culinary training frighten you. I know how to cook the fancy stuff, but I really prefer simple and tasty meals. I've found that most people feel the same way when it comes to food. I look forward to getting to know all of you." I smiled and nodded at the table to signal the end of my speech.

Only half a second passed before Anne took over once more. "Great. Okay. I'm going to introduce Sydney to everyone. All of you just sit back and wave when I call your name so she knows who is who. We can deal with more thorough introductions later. I'm starving."

Anne took a breath, reached behind her to grab my hand and pull me closer, and began pointing quickly around the room.

"We'll start on the left side. The empty seat there is for you, followed by—you already know Callum and Cooper—next to them is Cooper's mother, Grace, her husband, Eoghanan, Cooper's father, Jeffrey, and his wife Kathleen…"

The names went on and on. Despite my skill at remembering, there were so many in attendance that I feared a few of them would slip my mind from time to time. I made special note of the woman named Morna who sat at the end opposite to where I stood. She intrigued me more than anyone else.

With Callum's warning that she was mad, I expected her to look very different. She wasn't the eccentric, frazzled, elderly-looking woman that I had imagined, and she didn't appear to be out of her mind in the slightest. Instead, I felt like she looked into my soul with the clarity of her stare.

She was older than the others at the table, but she looked far younger than her husband. The beauty of her youth hadn't faded. Gray hair suited her, and she exuded an ethereal quality that made me realize why Cooper had seen fit to cast her as the witch in his story, though I would be very much surprised if she was indeed crazy as Callum suggested. She held herself with a sense of poise and grace that those riddled with memory problems did not.

When Anne ended what seemed like an endless stream of introductions, a collective laugh spread through the room as a great many of those in attendance wished me luck remembering a single one of them.

The woman nearest me reached out to squeeze my hand in greeting. "Doona worry. None one of us will be offended if ye call us a name other than our own."

I looked over at Blaire, smiling at the sight of her pregnant belly. I remembered her name not only due to her pregnancy, but also because of the similarity in both appearance and name she bore to the girl, Bri. I assumed they were twins.

"Good," I said with a laugh. "I'm glad no offense will be taken, but I will do my utmost to figure out who's who by the end of the week."

Blaire smiled and laughed, her pregnant belly lifting with each chuckle. "I used to know everyone's name, but it seems this babe has stolen my brain, for I forget names all the time now. I hear it's common during pregnancy. Go ahead and sit so we can eat. This babe has me hungry all the time."

With that, everyone started to fill their plates with food, and the casual atmosphere around the room made it effortless for me to feel at ease among them. There were two empty seats at the table—one next to Callum and another next to Morna. I didn't wish to sit next to either of them. Morna's gaze made me hesitant —I didn't think her eyes had left me since I entered the room— and I knew what sort of danger I was placing myself in if I sat next to Callum.

Deciding on my best course of action, I walked over to the empty seat next to Callum and leaned around him to tap Cooper on the shoulder. "Hey, you want to sit next to me? You're the only one at this table that I've had much of a chance to visit with. It might make me less nervous if you did so."

The young boy jumped up from his seat almost immediately, quickly tugging on Callum's chair to get him to stand. "You heard the lady, switch with me."

Callum looked back at me over his shoulder, winked teasingly at me, and then did as Cooper bid. It amused him that I didn't wish to sit next to him. For some reason, this playful side of him only made him more attractive to me, which in turn made me all the more aggravated.

Once Cooper was seated, I joined him, waiting until most everyone's plate was filled before reaching in to do the same with my own. The moment I brought the first bite to my lips, Morna's voice echoed from across the table.

"Ye are a fine cook, Sydney. I believe we are all pleased to have ye here. Do ye mind if I ask ye a few questions so that we may all get to know ye better?"

After my experience with Callum in the kitchen, I did mind very much, but of course, I meant to say that I didn't mind at all. Much to my horror, it didn't seem to matter what I meant. What I thought was what came out. "Yes, actually, I do mind."

Morna laughed, and her grin made my stomach churn uncomfortably. She looked as if she expected my answer to be just that, and it seemed to please her that she'd been right. "I'll make them quick," she said. "First . . . do ye believe in magic?"

I pulled my brows together and glanced around the table, expecting everyone to regard Morna with the same baffled expression as my own. Instead, everyone looked blankly in my direction, waiting for my response. "No," I said slowly. "I don't think I do. Why? That seems like a very strange question."

No one else said a word, and I got the feeling that they were under orders not to. Morna was the only one who spoke.

"I suppose it does seem strange," she agreed. "Next question: Do ye or have ye ever known or had contact with the witch named Grier?"

It was the same name Jerry had mentioned to me before. "No, I definitely have not. Did you just say witch?"

"Aye, lass. I said witch. Ye will become quite familiar with the word this evening."

"Your husband asked me about Grier, as well. Does she live here? I confess to being rather confused."

Morna flinched. "My husband? Jerry?"

For the first time since my entry into the dining hall, Morna's expression looked less than calm. My words had surprised her. I wondered why. "Yes, Jerry. When I helped him carry a plate of food up to his room, he asked me if I knew anyone named Grier. Should I?"

"No. You shouldna. I'm glad that ye doona. Back to Jerry—ye carried food to his room? I thought he dinna come down to dinner because he dinna feel well. Do ye know why he's not here? Did he tell you?"

Any normal night I would have told her it was none of my business and she should ask him herself. But tonight, I blurted out exactly what had taken place. "He's upset with you, but he didn't go into specifics. He did ask me about someone named Grier though, and then he told me that he was sorry if this dinner didn't go well for me."

Morna's face grew pale, but the revelation didn't slow her interrogation of me. "I've one last question for ye. Forgive me for its personal nature, but I need to make certain the spell worked."

As my confusion deepened, Callum interrupted, saying, "Morna, ye doona need to embarrass the lass. I assure ye I made certain the spell was still in effect only a few moments ago. I swear to ye, it is."

I silently watched their exchange as my mind reeled from the oddity of it all.

"Ye dinna spell me, Morna," Callum continued. "So I'm under no obligation to tell ye what I asked her or her response."

"Verra well." I could sense Morna's words even before she spoke them. "Sydney, what did Callum ask ye?"

In one brief moment of genius it occurred to me that silence wasn't a lie. I could ignore her question. I could refuse to answer it without embarrassing myself further. I couldn't make sense of what was happening to me or with this conversation, but I could at least hold on to that.

I took a breath. "You know what, I don't want to be impolite on my first day here, but I think I'm finished talking to you for now. Let's let everyone finish the meal. I won't be answering any more questions."

Four seats down from me, the woman Anne had called Jane spoke up in my defense. "Morna, don't look so disappointed that she's smart and figured out how to avoid your harassment. Surely Sydney has answered enough questions for us to be certain that she doesn't know anything. If Callum says he's sure the spell took, then I believe him. Look at her. I can't even imagine what she must be thinking about us after being asked about witches and us talking about spells. She's not used to this."

"What are you thinking?"

The question came from Cooper, and as the attention in the room turned to me once again, I decided not to ignore this particular question. "Since I've apparently been slipped some sort of truth serum..." The bitter coffee flashed through my mind, and I paused and turned to glance down at Cooper. "The coffee. It was the coffee, wasn't it?"

He nodded and reached out to squeeze my arm apologetically. "Yeah, but I'm so sorry. I didn't know. I promise, I didn't. I drank some of it, too. Remember? It's been like the worst day ever. Usually when my little sister asks me if I want to play dolls with her, I either lie and say yes, or I pretend I'm really tired or something. Today when she asked, I told her that I'd rather watch my favorite dinosaur toy get flushed down the toilet than play with her dolls. She cried for half an hour."

"Right." I glanced away from him and back to the group. "Anyway, as I was saying. Since I've been drugged—I refuse to say spelled since, let's get real, that's not a thing—I'm thinking that no matter how beautiful the castle, no matter how attractive the males are around here, that I've made a terrible mistake in coming here. As far as I can see, there are only two possible scenarios here. The first being that this is some sort of initiation skit, and if that's the case, it's so juvenile I'm not sure I want to work in that sort of environment. The second is that there's a gas leak somewhere in the castle, and it's slowly been poisoning you all, and you've gone and lost your minds. Either way, I should be gathering my things."

I took a deep breath as I finished. It was only through saying the words out loud that I realized how truly frightened I was. Earlier in the kitchen with Callum, I had somehow justified my answers to him by rationalizing that perhaps my subconscious had wanted me to answer him truthfully so maybe he would kiss me. But this? Morna was intentionally asking me strange questions because she believed I couldn't lie to her. And the topic of conversation as a whole was the strangest thing I'd ever sat through in my entire life.

Morna surprised me by standing and walking the long distance around the table, only stopping when she stood directly behind me. She leaned in, placing both hands on my shoulders as she spoke quietly near my ear. "I'm sorry for what I've done to ye, but I'm afraid I feel it more important that I speak with my husband than explain everything to ye. If he mentioned Grier to ye, then something I dinna intend has happened. The others will tell ye everything."

She made it nearly to the doors before Callum stood and called out to her. "Are ye convinced now, Morna? Can we end this and tell her so she's no longer frightened and confused? Can ye promise me ye'll treat her the same as ye do all of us now?"

Morna turned and smiled gently in my direction. "Aye, Callum. Tell her everything. I believe her. I like her verra much. She's as fiery as every lass I ever brought to ye bunch of rowdy men. I only wish I knew why Grier sent the email. The wondering of it is not good on my nerves, and now that Jerry knows, I only hope his heart can stand it. "

"Morna. Wait." The second voice was Cooper's. I turned to see him climbing up so that he stood in his chair. "Grier didn't send the email."

"How do ye know that, lad?"

I didn't have a clue what any of them were talking about, but I could see the hope in her eyes.

"I know because I was the one who sent it."

"You what?" The question was echoed by at least three other voices around the room.

"Yeah, I was playing on Anne's computer in the office a few weeks ago, and I accidentally saw it, and then my stomach growled, and I thought about eating more frozen pizza or another one of her meals, and I just thought maybe it would be a good idea to send it and see if Sydney showed up. And she did, and her food is great, so there's no problem, right? I'm not in trouble?"

Morna ran over to the boy, scooped him up in her arms, and planted kisses all over his face.

"Cooper, after what I put ye through today, I wouldna get on to ye about anything. I couldna be more pleased that it was ye, and not Grier, responsible for Sydney's arrival."

She set Cooper down on his feet and then came over and wrapped her arms around me in a tight embrace.

"I'm sorry, lass. I'm sorry for so many things. I hope with time ye'll come to think differently of me than ye do right now. Welcome to Cagair Castle. If ye'll open yer mind and yer heart, ye will find many special things here."

CHAPTER 15

*I*n the short moments following Morna's departure from the dining hall, Callum watched Sydney closely. She didn't appear frightened, but he knew she must be.

The entire room was silent, everyone waiting for her to speak. Eventually, rather than reward their silence, she stood and walked from the room without a word.

He waited a moment to give her time to exit the dining hall, then rose to follow her. "Sydney, wait," he called after her as she took the stairs upward, two at a time, to the castle's second level. With his leg still tender, he would never be able to catch her. When she stopped and spun toward him, he exhaled in relief that he wouldn't have to try. He didn't want her to see him limp or wonder why it took so long for him to follow.

"Callum, what is going on?" she demanded.

They walked toward each other, and he didn't answer until they met mid-way down the curved staircase in the main entryway.

"I'll tell ye every bit of it, lass, and I swear every word will be true. I'm sorry for all of it. I'm sorry if it upset ye, if ye are frightened or confused. 'Tis something every lassie at that table has experienced in one way or another. It just seems to be the way of it."

She pointed at him, stepping close enough that the tip of her finger lightly touched the center of his chest. Her hand trembled against him. He wanted nothing more than to gather her up in his arms to comfort her, but he refrained from doing so—she was too upset for that now.

Blinking at him, she said, "See? All of that strange stuff that you all keep saying—what does it mean? 'Every lassie?' Every girl at that table has been drugged and toyed with their first night here? If so, why did they stay? I need answers, Callum. Lots of them."

"I know ye do. And I will give them to you. Grab yer coat and come with me. I need to show ye something outside."

He waited for her, and he hoped with every passing second that she would take it well. It was a difficult thing for all of them, but he found the men of his own time—a time where magic was often believed and sought—accepted it a little easier than all of the modern lassies he'd grown to know and love. Eventually, though, they all adjusted. Surely Sydney would do the same. He didn't want her to take the second vial he held in his grasp, and he didn't want her to leave the castle.

He wanted her to stay and to know and accept the truth of it all. He wanted time to get to know her better.

"I'm ready. Let's go." She walked right past him when she returned, not waiting for his direction on where he meant for them to go. Once outside, she faced him. "Okay. Spill."

He reached for her arm, and he smiled when she allowed him to take it. Slowly, he walked her further away from the castle. "I want ye to see the whole castle, every bit of it, so ye will easily see the difference between this time and the last."

"Oh, for the love of—can can you people quit it with the strange references to things that don't make any sense?"

"Sydney . . ." He paused and reached to pull her chin upward so that she looked him right in the eyes. "Ye'll understand all of it in a moment, but ye must stop going on about it first. Just listen."

She huffed and pulled away from him, crossing her arms as they stared up at the castle together. The full moon shone brightly behind it, illuminating the silhouette of every tower and peak.

"Okay, Callum. I won't say another word if you start talking now. I promise. What are we looking at?"

He knew it would be a miracle if she truly stayed silent long enough for him to tell her what he needed to. She wouldn't believe a thing until he took her to his own time. "I want ye to take notice of everything. Ye see the tower in the back? 'Tis full and not crumbling. The lights in front are electric. The cars in front, many. Aye?"

He grinned to himself as she nodded. Even after asking a question, she stayed true to her promise.

"Earlier, when Cooper told ye what ye thought was a story— his talk of the magic, Morna's witchcraft, the staircase leading to the past—'tis all true. In the year sixteen hundred and fifty, Cagair Castle belongs to me. Many of those ye dined with this evening were also born and live in that time."

Her face remained unchanged at his words. If anything, he thought she looked bored.

"Sydney, did ye not hear what I just said?"

"I did hear. I'm just trying to figure out how far and long I will have to run until I get to the nearest town and can escape you crazies. I'm sure it's far, but I'm a great runner. Truly, even if it's thirty miles away, I can make it."

He laughed, making certain to keep hold of her arm lest she truly try to run. "I've no doubt of it. Ye are tight as a bow string, and ye've not an ounce of stuffing on ye. Do ye wish to see proof that I'm not mad? I'll take ye to my time if ye will allow it."

"Please, do take me. But if we get near that staircase and it ends up being some sort of cage or trap, you should know that

I've taken self-defense classes. It doesn't matter that you are nearly three times my size, I swear I will kick your butt. Got it?"

Every new thing that came out of her mouth made him like her more. "Aye, lass. I have most assuredly 'got it.' Come this way."

The lamps around the castle illuminated the path. When they reached the top of the staircase, enough light exposed the steps so they could see the stone wall at the bottom. He knew it would be difficult to coax her to enter.

"It's stone, Callum. I'm not walking down those steps just to bang straight into a wall of stone. Is this all for you to get a good laugh? Are you trying to see how gullible I am? Because I'm not. At this point, I'm just placating you while I try to figure out a plan of escape."

"Ye are not a prisoner here. If ye wish to leave, ye are free to do so. I hope that ye will not."

He gauged her reaction carefully. He didn't think she would run, but it was difficult to tell with the way she kept continually glancing back over her shoulder.

"You have to go first," she said after some time. "If you walk to the bottom and don't smack your nose right up against that wall, I will follow you."

He didn't know if she would actually follow him, but he didn't plan to haul her down the staircase against her will. If she wanted to come, she would have to do so on her own. The decision would be hers.

Callum nodded. "Fine. Ye'll see me disappear. When ye do, walk down the steps and doona hesitate to walk straight through. Ye'll find no resistance at the bottom of the stairs."

"Right. I'm sure that I won't."

Her voice was filled with disbelief, but he thought her eyes reflected more wonder than skepticism. It caused hope to rise within him. Surely, once she saw everything with her own eyes, her resistance and fear would fade.

Callum gave Sydney a quick smile then took the steps downward. Before he stepped through, he turned his head to watch her eyes as he disappeared.

The shock was evident. And he knew with certainty that Sydney would follow him.

CHAPTER 16

1 650

I only allowed a few seconds to pass after Callum disappeared at the bottom of the stairwell before I ran down the steps after him. I intended to stop short of the wall, to reach out and touch it slowly, but my proximity must have been too close, for some force pulled me through.

When I opened my eyes in the same spot I'd stood a moment before, the first difference I noticed was the darkness. My logical mind still demanded I deny the possibility of truth here, but it was undeniably dark in the stairwell. The same moon still shone, but no traces of electricity illuminated my path.

I felt my way upward, looking toward the top to see Callum's hand reaching downward to guide me out of the cellar-like entrance.

"Let's go to the front of the castle," he said.

It was the first thing I wanted to see. After all, it was the whole reason he'd made me look at its silhouette only moments ago. He wanted me to see the difference.

Within ten feet, while I kept moving my feet forward, I knew I didn't need to see the front to know that all of it was somehow remarkably true. The cars were gone, the lamp posts nonexistent, and the silence in the air was almost eerie in its palpability.

"All right, lass. Turn around."

I did as he asked. I enjoyed the feeling of his arms wrapping around my back, although I knew he only did so to point ahead of me and draw my attention to the shape of the castle.

Sure enough, it was very different. The tower at the back was only half there.

I twisted in his arms, and he took a half step away from me. I was no longer angry, no longer scared, just immensely curious and intrigued.

"Okay. You have my full attention. How is this possible?"

He jerked his head toward the castle doors, and I walked next to him, eager to see its interior.

"I canna tell ye how 'tis possible, for I doona know, but I'll tell ye what I can. It'll be dark, Sydney. The windows are few until we reach the tower. I'll lead ye straight there. Do ye mind if I take yer hand?"

"Please do. I'd rather not stumble around in the dark."

The touch of his hand warmed me right through, and I felt safe as he led me through the darkened halls of the castle.

"I doona wish to take the time to light a torch," said Callum. "When we reach the tower, the walls still standing will block the wind, and the moon will be bright enough for us to see."

I tried to make out as much as I could in the darkness, glancing this way and that for the possible sight of a light switch or an outlet, but as far as I could tell, none existed. He walked quickly, but I had no trouble keeping pace. When we reached the tower, it took a moment for my eyes to adjust to the moon's brightness.

"I don't think I've ever seen the moon put off so much light."

"Aye, I agree. I doona know why, but it seems 'tis brighter in this time. Come and sit now that ye are not so ready to flee. I'm glad that ye dinna leave me standing on this side of time all alone."

He continued to hold onto my hands as he spoke, gently rubbing them to keep me warm. We couldn't have been in the crumbling tower for more than half an hour, but in that time, he told me more than I ever would have expected to learn.

Everything about the fire, the wretch of a man who set it, how he knew Morna and her strong connection with nearly everyone staying at Cagair in the present, and finally, Grier, the mysterious witch who helped him so many months ago. I asked little as he spoke, intent to soak up every word he wanted to share. When he finished, he gave my hands a gentle squeeze.

"What are ye thinking, lass?"

"So many things. I'm sorry for the fire—for the pain it caused you, for the lives lost in it. I can see in your eyes how speaking of it still hurts you."

His eyes widened at my words. I guessed he expected me to question rather than console him. I'm sure I would have questions later, but for now, my mind was too filled with processing everything he'd said.

"It does, but I was lucky. It only pains me that I was not here to keep the others safe. Had I not been absent, Macaslan would've taken his anger out on me, not those innocent people. I would've made certain, even if it cost my own life."

I scooted closer to him, every inch of me wanting to have him near. "If not for you, Nora would've died in that fire. There's no way to know that you could have kept Macaslan from hurting the others. There's no looking back from things like that. You just have to move forward."

"Aye, ye are right." He stood, still grasping my hand. "'Tis time to go. I doona think it wise to be here without others around."

He took the path out of the castle more slowly, and it seemed to me that he couldn't decide whether or not he actually wanted to leave. He slowed his pace even more as we approached the passageway adjacent to the bedrooms, and I spoke out to him in the darkness.

"Callum, I wasn't cold in the tower if that's what you were worried about. It's all right with me if you want to stay a while longer. You seem to be taking the long way out of the castle." I laughed teasingly, knowing full well what it looked like for a person to drag their feet. For the last year of running the restaurant, it seemed I was doing it all the time.

He laughed as well, but it didn't match my own laughter. His was deeper, more strained. When he spoke in the darkness, I jumped at the nearness of his voice, not having seen him lean in close.

"I'm glad ye think me so noble, lass, but I dinna fear for yer warmth. I knew that if I looked into yer eyes a moment longer, I would not be able to hide my feelings for you."

Memories of our time in the kitchen flooded my mind. I wanted him to kiss me, and he knew it. I didn't understand his hesitation.

"Why would you hide it?"

"I've not even known ye a day, Sydney, but from the first moment I laid eyes on ye, I've wanted nothing more than to hold ye against me and kiss ye until the only breath ye can breathe is my own. Do ye still wish me to kiss ye?"

With Morna's potion still in full effect, my answer slipped out immediately. In that moment, I knew that I would answer the same way even without it.

"Yes."

His hands moved to cup either side of my face. Although I could not see him, I could feel his breath against my neck.

"I'll kiss ye, lass, but not this night—not when Morna's potion still courses through yer veins. I wish to kiss ye when ye have the power to say no even if you do want me to kiss you."

He didn't step away, and I used the opportunity to lean forward and press my lips against his. The potion had no influence on my behavior. If I wanted to kiss him, I didn't think for a moment that he would object.

He didn't.

He pulled me tight against him, backing me into the nearest wall. His lips were soft and warm against my own. He allowed the kiss to continue for a long moment before he pulled away, grabbed my hand, and took off at a remarkably fast rate toward the main doors of the castle.

"Well, I dinna expect ye to do that, lass."

I had to run to keep up with him, but I didn't mind. Running was never a problem, but with the endorphins flowing through me, it was a breeze.

"Do you wish that I hadn't?" I asked breathlessly.

He laughed and, once we were outside, turned toward me. This time he leaned in, kissing me quickly and gently on the lips before pulling away to gaze at me in the moonlight. "No, I'm glad ye did, though it only makes me hope even more that ye willna take what I have to offer ye. I doona wish to be the only one to remember that come morning."

"What do you mean?"

He bent and retrieved a small glass bottle from the top of his boot. "Doona worry. I can see ye cringe, even if ye do yer best to hide it. 'Tis not a truth potion. Morna gave it to me to offer ye in case, after learning the truth, ye dinna wish to know it. If ye drink this before bed, ye will wake remembering nothing of this night. Yer knowledge of the magic that goes on here will be gone."

Surely, he didn't think I would want to forget all of this, but I appreciated the gesture all the same. It placed the choice in my hands, and that was something I'd had very little of today. "Thank you."

He nodded, slipped it into my hand, and turned to walk back toward the staircase. "Let me lead ye back, lass. Doona tell me whether ye plan to take it or not. Ye should think on it all first. Ye should know that if ye drink of this vial, yer ignorance of the magic will keep me away. I wouldna wish to be the one to upset yer world. I'm sure 'tis plenty bonny without me in it. But, Sydney, if ye decide not to take it, if ye know the truth, I'll want ye with me every moment of every day. And I intend to pursue ye most ardently."

CHAPTER 17

*P*resent Day

*M*orna sighed, obviously exasperated. "She might already be sleeping, Jerry. After a day like she's had, I'm sure she's tired enough to sleep for a month."

"I doona care if she's sleeping. If ye wish to get in bed with me this night, ye will apologize to the lass this instant. I mean it, Morna. I am finished with all of this. I willna have ye acting like a child a moment longer, and if ye put poppies in my drink again, I'll be putting arsenic in yers. Do ye understand me, woman?"

I stood cautiously at my door, listening for the moment when either of them took a breath long enough for me to open up and show them that I was, in fact, still awake.

They carried on that way for nearly five minutes, bickering back and forth, Jerry giving Morna quite a mouthful. It made me like the man immensely.

I jumped at the quick rap of knuckles on my door, but I

waited a few seconds to open it so it wouldn't seem like I'd been standing there listening the entire time.

When I opened up, Jerry immediately leaned in for a hug while Morna stood back, looking at me with guilty eyes.

"Did we wake ye, Sydney?" she murmured. "I told Jerry we shouldna be coming to yer room this time of night."

"No, you didn't wake me. Not at all. I've got a lot on my mind. I doubt I will sleep a wink."

Jerry pulled away from me and gave Morna a quick stare, undoubtedly intended to get her to apologize. She did just that.

"I know a lot of what is on yer mind is my fault, and I apologize for the day ye've had. I'm ashamed of the way I treated ye. There is no reason for it. I canna imagine how confused and frightened ye must be. Did Callum give ye the other potion?"

I still held it in my hands, and I lifted it so she could see it.

"Yes. He did. You don't need to apologize, Morna. I understand." I knew that was a gross understatement. Thirty minutes of conversation, while revealing, still left me many paces behind everyone else. "Well, at least I understand more than I did. I can't say I would've acted differently had I been in your shoes."

Jerry didn't wait for an invitation before stepping inside my bedroom. "See, Morna? Was that so difficult? I told ye the lass would take it well. She's far more kind than ye are." He turned away from his wife and directed his attention at me. "Will ye take the potion, lass?"

I didn't know. Callum alone was enough to make me want to toss the thing, but my decision involved so much more than him. Was I comfortable being privy to such knowledge of magic? If I spent my life around those so accustomed to it, would I ever be fully in control of my own life again?

"I don't know. Should I?"

Jerry didn't answer me right away, instead turning to usher Morna from the room.

"Ye've said yer apology. Go and get in our bed and warm it up for me. I wish to speak to the lass alone."

She bid me a quick farewell and left us. Jerry spoke the moment he closed the door behind her. "I dinna want to speak in front of her. She's too involved with the magic to give ye a fair answer. I'll tell ye, instead, what I know to be true for myself."

I moved to a small chair and motioned for him to do the same.

"That sounds great. I'd love to hear what you think."

"Doona take it. Flush it and doona think twice about doing so. Anyone who knows me will tell ye that my feelings about magic are not all good. It frightens me for more reasons than I wish to share with ye now, and it always has. Not only that, but I've spent most of my life witnessing how the burden of magic has impacted my wife. 'Tis not an easy thing to be able to see, and sense, and change things in ways that others canna. Magic is a responsibility that not all can bear. But the knowing of magic, well that is rather extraordinary. It makes us a few out of millions. I, for one, wouldna change that for anything in the world."

He yawned—a big, long, wide yawn that passed right over to me the moment it ended. We laughed together at our shared fatigue.

"That is my opinion of it, lass, but if ye decide to take it, not a one of us will blame ye. I best be on my way. I've been angry with my wife for far too long. I'm eager to make up with her." He grinned slyly, and his cheeks blushed in a way that made me chuckle as I walked him to the door.

"Thank you, Jerry. I hope we will be good friends. I'm going to go toss this thing the moment I close this door."

He gave me a quick peck on the cheek and stepped into the hallway.

"I'm pleased to hear it. Ye doona need to hope, lass, we are already bonny friends."

I smiled and closed the door before marching straight to the bathroom where I uncorked the small vial and poured the thick, rose-colored liquid down the drain.

For years I'd been desperate for something to change in my life. Now it had.

I wouldn't be turning back for anything.

CHAPTER 18

It was still completely dark. Why on earth would the lass have need to run before the sun was even up? Callum couldn't see the sense of it, especially when he knew how tired Sydney must be after arriving in Scotland only yesterday. To think of everything that had occurred in only a day made his own head spin. Most people would sleep in at least for a bit after such an eventful day. If rising at this time of morning was considered "sleeping in" for her, he knew she had to be an even greater insomniac than wee Cooper.

The only thing that allowed him to see Sydney at all in such darkness was the light attached to her forehead. He recognized the contraption as one of Aiden's tools, and he knew she must've borrowed it so she would be able to see the path ahead of her as she ran. It was smart thinking, for there were a number of holes that he wouldn't wish to come across in the dark if he were traipsing about at such an hour.

Callum was only up at such an early hour due to the castle's pressing restorations. This had been his schedule for the past few months. Normally, he preferred to wake up naturally, when it was light outside.

"She's a beauty, aye?"

Morna's voice startled him, causing him to jump at the unexpected noise, his forehead bumping into the window glass with enough force to elicit an apology from the old witch.

"Ach, I'm sorry, I should've made myself known as I approached."

"What are ye doing up?" Callum asked, rubbing the spot just above his eyebrow. "I dinna wake ye, did I? I made no effort to be quiet, but I thought the tower to be far enough from every other room that there was no fear of me waking anyone."

"Oh goodness, no. Ye dinna wake me. The older I get, the less I sleep. I doona mind it, though. I enjoy being up when most are still asleep. It's peaceful, aye?"

"Aye, though not peaceful enough to keep me waking at this hour once the castle is restored."

Morna reached up and squeezed his shoulder gently. "All of ye lads have worked so hard these past months. Ye all need to sleep to yer heart's content once ye finish."

Even if Morna usually did wake early, he'd never seen her up on any other morning as he and the other men readied to head down the stairwell. There was undoubtedly a reason for her being here now.

"What is it, Morna?" Tilting his head to one side, he squinted at her. "I can see there is something ye mean to say. Best get on with it. I've not much time before I need to join the others for a long day of work."

"I know ye'll be busy. With most of ye cutting yer work day short yesterday so everyone could meet Sydney, ye've time to make up today. I thought perhaps this would be the only chance I'd have to catch ye alone to tell ye that I spoke with the lass last night after ye returned. She was verra amenable to my apology, and seemed to take everything quite well. I believe Jerry convinced her to not drink the potion. I promise ye that I'll not use nor offer magic to the girl again."

He hoped very much that Morna was right about Sydney and the potion. It would be so much easier for all of them if she knew the truth. He didn't want her to forget anything that had occurred between them. "I'm glad to hear it, Morna, but 'tis not me ye should be telling. Ye should tell Sydney herself that ye'll not be using magic on her again."

"I did. I also decided that I am finished wasting my time or energy worrying about Grier. I still believe we will all have to deal with her now that I know she's alive, but I willna sacrifice my marriage just so I can worry about what has yet to happen. Jerry was verra forthright with me after I tracked him down last night. I doona think he's ever been so angry with me. He is not well, and I'll not upset him more than need be. He's demanded I stop, so I shall."

"But...?" Callum knew she wasn't finished. If she was, she wouldn't be pacing around the tower nervously.

She paused to grin at him. "Ye know me too well. I shouldna say what I'm about to, but I shall. I was simply going to say that Jerry made me swear *I* will stop worrying about Grier and stop preparing spells to use against her. I willna break my word, but I gave him no promise that anyone else should stop. Will ye look for her, Callum? I'll not do anything myself, and I'll not show Jerry my worry, but I canna bear not knowing what she wants."

Callum very much wanted to find Grier himself, not just for Morna, but for the sake of his own potent curiosity. Ever since the day of the fire, he'd not stopped wondering about her. But with so much time already passed since he saw her, he doubted his ability to track her down. If she didn't want to be found, he didn't imagine she would be. He would look for her, to be certain, but he thought it best Morna remain ignorant of his searching. He didn't want her wondering and worrying about Grier unless he succeeded.

He crossed his arms. "Why, ye have changed yer tune, have ye not, Morna? Only a few days ago, ye warned me that she planned to interfere with my life and that I shouldna dare her to do so."

"Callum." Morna looked at him as if she thought him dense. "She already has. Can ye not tell by now?"

"Doona tell me ye are still suspicious of Sydney?"

"No, I've no concern over the lass at all, but that doesna mean that Grier has not already interfered. 'Tis no coincidence that Cooper emailed the woman ye saw so many months ago. I've not told anyone this, but 'twas Grier who first gave me a taste for matching others with their mates, though this one is not my doing."

"Ye think Grier means to match me with Sydney?" Callum could see no reason that the old witch would want to do any such thing, but what could it possibly hurt? "If so, it seems a harmless way to interfere with my life. I like Sydney verra much. I think perhaps Jerry is right that we shouldna think of Grier another moment." He shook his head. "I'm sorry, but no, I will not go look for her. Not now. If something else occurs that gives us cause to, I will consider yer request then."

Morna sighed. "Verra well. Perhaps 'tis for the best. I willna press ye." She stood and left him without another word.

Only once he heard Morna greet someone inside the stairwell did he realize why she'd accepted his denial of her request so easily. She didn't want to be overheard. If not for the approaching visitor, she would have given him a much harder time about it.

He stood and waited to see who approached, smiling when Anne appeared in the doorway. Save Jane, Morna, and Jerry, Anne was Callum's closest friend at the castle.

"Callum, can I ask you about something?" asked Anne."

"Aye, of course."

"Gillian and I have been talking. We have an idea, and I'd like your opinion"

Nothing made him more anxious than the thought of one of Anne's "ideas." While well meaning, it was sure to mean more work and time for everyone. "I doona know why ye would seek my approval about such matters, Anne. I am but a guest in the Cagair of this time. Anything ye and Gillian decide is fine, for 'tis yer castle."

"I know, but this will affect you more than most of the things we decide. We've been working on it for a while now, actually. It's a party of sorts."

"A party?" Everything in him churned uncomfortably at the thought. A party would mean much more work indeed.

"Yes, a party. I don't know if you realize it, but tomorrow will be six months to the day since the castle fire. Everyone's been working so hard, there's been very little else happening. I think we all could use an excuse to relax and have a good time. I've heard several of you talk of how your men at the original Cagair are always asking if they can travel forward to see what it's like here. It would be the perfect excuse to give them all a thrill."

He couldn't deny that all who sacrificed so much in service of him were due a good time. On second thought, perhaps that wasn't the only reason a dance wouldn't be the worst thing in the world. Such an event might give him the perfect opportunity to seek out Grier.

Morna once told him that she didn't believe Grier would travel forward. But as far as Callum could tell, Grier wasn't interested in anyone that traveled into the past daily. If she was, he would have seen her since the fire. No, if she remained close to Cagair Castle, it was for Morna, and Callum knew Morna was dead set against ever returning to the time in which she'd been born. If Morna wouldn't come to Grier, why was it so far-fetched to believe that if they gave Grier the opportunity, the old witch might come to Morna? Callum truly believed none of them would find peace until whatever it was between the two witches was settled.

It would be difficult for Grier to travel forward without being noticed on most days, but if they held a party, perhaps she would be tempted to come since she could more easily stay hidden among the workers and their families.

It wasn't a bad idea. More than that—it was the only idea he could think of that might actually work.

"Hello? You there?" Anne widened her eyes. "Did you hear a thing I said?"

Anne's irritated voice pulled him from his thoughts. "Ach, sorry. Aye, I did hear ye. I think it a grand idea. I believe I'll wait to tell my men until the end of work today, though. Otherwise, they willna get a thing done."

"How was your run, Sydney?" Anne asked. "I must say, I was very surprised to see you up so early. You looked so tired when you arrived yesterday. I planned to leave breakfast outside your room."

I stepped through the front door of the castle to Anne's warm greeting. I still wore her husband's task light and sheepishly took it off my head. Handing it to her, I said, "The run was great. I hope it's okay that I borrowed Aiden's light. I should have asked someone before taking it, but everyone was still asleep. I didn't want to wake anyone. It was lying right by the back door, and it seemed a pretty good idea."

Anne laughed and waved a dismissive hand before leading me down the hallway. "Aiden won't mind at all that you borrowed it. Feel free to take it with you each day. It was a brilliant idea to do so. Truly. You can't imagine how many holes there are out there. We get so much rain that it's a big problem. That's the sort of task we've left for last. Within the next few weeks, someone will be out to work on the road leading to the castle."

I followed along behind her slowly, taking deep breaths to slow my heart rate with each new step. "Thank you. The light really helped. I'm afraid I would've twisted an ankle without it." My gaze skimmed over each nook and cranny of the castle's interior as we passed by. "This is truly a stunning property, Anne."

"It is, isn't it?"

We paused only briefly at the top of the stairs leading to the kitchen below. Then Anne hurried down them, pulling me along behind her. When we reached the bottom, I was shocked to see the pastries I'd placed in the oven before my run out on the counter, perfectly dusted with powdered sugar.

"Did you do that?" I asked Anne.

She reached for one of the sugary treats, then hopped up to sit on the edge of the counter. I didn't have the heart to tell her she'd landed right in a pile of scattered sugar. I figured she would find that out for herself once she stood.

"No, Morna did it," she said, speaking with her mouth full. "It seems you aren't the only one of us who rose early this morning. I think she's trying to make up for everything she put you through yesterday."

I gave my hands a quick wash and reached for a pastry, which I held in one hand while I worked to wipe down the messy counters with the other. "Well, remind me to thank her the next time I see her."

"Sure." Anne wiped sugar from her mouth with the back of her hand. "Speaking of Morna and everything else...how are you doing?"

I knew right away what her real question was. She was testing me to see if I remembered anything. She wanted to know if I had drunk the potion. "I'm pretty good. It's not every day a girl learns she's staying in a magical castle and that witches exist."

Anne's smile was contagious. "Oh, I'm so glad you didn't take Morna's potion! It will be great not to have to tiptoe around you, and I wasn't really sure how all of that was going to work anyway with all of the men going back and forth every day. You would catch on pretty fast."

"Yes," I agreed, "I suppose I would. It seemed pretty pointless to forget something that I would only have to learn of eventually anyway. I know it's only my second day here, but I hope to stay a long time. I think I'm really going to love it. I suppose it's best that I get used to the new normal of my life sooner rather than later, yes?"

"Absolutely. I've not actually ever been back in time myself. But through watching everyone else, I've come to believe that the magic only reveals itself to those of us who can handle it. We modern women have adjusted pretty well to the oddity of it all."

Taking the wet, crumb-filled rag over to the sink, I rinsed it and continued our conversation. "You really have. Why haven't you gone back, Anne?"

She shrugged. "Maybe I will someday. I've adjusted to the possibility of it, but that doesn't mean that it doesn't freak me out a little. I'd rather not travel to a place that doesn't give me immediate access to a flushable toilet." She laughed. "Besides, Aiden is here. He's not from the past like the rest of the men. I'm just happy to be where he is."

"I understand."

Studying my expression, she asked, "What did you think of it?"

"It was hard to see much of anything, it was so dark. But I could certainly see enough to know that you all were telling me the truth. Callum sort of rushed us back. He didn't seem to want me there very long."

"I'm not surprised. With Laird Macaslan still missing, Callum is very protective of us. He likes great numbers of people present there at all times. In fact, that's the main reason I expected him to say no to the idea of a party. I still can't believe he said yes."

"Party?" Anne knew that she'd not told me about it, but I didn't care that she was fishing for me to ask her more questions.

"Yes. I was a little nervous to tell you since you just started and everything. But don't worry, Morna promised me that she will help. She's quite a good cook. I should've allowed her to take over the kitchen a long time ago, but I just have too much pride, I suppose.

"Anyway, we're having a big party here tomorrow night to bring some joy and life back into this place. It's been too filled with work and stress. Gillian and I decided that the food and dress will remain traditional so as not to completely take everyone that will be attending out of their comfort zone. But we will leave the use of all modern conveniences available for our guests to explore."

"So, I'm assuming these guests will not be from this time period then?" It was difficult for me to tell if Anne was being vague on purpose, or if her mind just moved so quickly that she often left out details when explaining things to others.

She smiled and slid off the counter, dragging a dusting of sugar down onto the floor. "That's the best part. Callum's agreed to let his workers and their families attend. Shortly after the fire, when all the clans arrived and Callum could see that he would need plenty of men to help him, he shared news of the magic with his village. So they all know. They've been begging him to let them see for themselves ever since."

Grabbing a broom to sweep up Anne's mess, I said, "That seems like a risky thing to do. What if news of the magic spreads to someone it shouldn't?"

Anne shrugged, apparently not sharing my concern. "If the fire showed Callum anything, it's that he can trust his people. And you have to understand that things are very different in the past. It doesn't even come as that much of a surprise to them. Many of that time period believe in magic and have witnessed it for themselves."

It all seemed so strange—that all of this could be discussed so easily, as if it were commonplace for everyone. I wondered then how it would change my life outside of my work here. Would I ever look at anything the same way again? With every strange occurrence or happenstance strike of luck, would I wonder if some unseen magic was involved? Would I ever be able to tell my own family? If not, could I learn to accept the burden of keeping such a secret from them?

All of them would love hearing it—my mom, my sister, my dad most of all. I could just see his amusement with it all. I could almost hear how embarrassing his words would be, how he would quote movie lines and don a kilt with such glee that everyone near him would think him crazy.

Learning of the magic was just the first bit of it, I supposed. Living with it and moving forward was another. There was still much I would have to sort out in my own mind and heart before this seemed normal.

My thoughts shifting to the party, I said, "So, what kind of menu do I need to draw up for tomorrow night? And how many do I need to feed?"

Anne bared her teeth, looking apprehensive. "I'm going to leave the menu up to you, but keep it simple. Meat, potatoes, wine, ale—everyone is really just going to want to come for the dancing. As far as the number, at least one hundred."

I swallowed quickly, hoping to dislodge my brief moment of panic so it wouldn't be heard in my voice. I could handle the large event, but I wouldn't be able to come up for air until the party started.

"All right, got it," I said, sounding calmer than I felt. "Can I borrow the car and a map? I definitely need to get some groceries."

650

*C*allum stood surrounded by all the able-bodied men in his village with the neighboring lairds gathered at his back. "I am pleased that ye are all so verra excited. We will start early and work until midday tomorrow. Then I'll allow ye all to return home to clean yerselves up and prepare yer families for the festivities. I hope ye all know how grateful I am for yer help."

Everyone seemed delighted at the thought of a party in the twenty-first century. As excitement spread throughout the group, Callum found himself looking forward to it as well. There was only one thing left to discuss with his men, and it was the most important thing he could ask.

"Before we end our work today, I wish to discuss safety measures for this gathering. All from the village are welcome. I doona believe Macaslan is in the country. Even if he is, he willna know of the magic here. Still, we must be on alert for him and his men. Enjoy yerselves, but keep watch amongst the crowds, aye?"

The collective ayes of agreement were all he needed to hear. The party would proceed as planned. If luck befell them, Grier would join the celebration as well.

CHAPTER 20

With Anne and Gillian completely overwhelmed with decorating and planning for the party, I was left to spend every spare minute making the meal preparations. The castle's kitchen was now my workspace, bedroom, and dining room as I worked around the clock to make certain everything was ready on time. Luckily, I didn't have to do it all alone. Morna and Jerry kept me company while serving as my cooking partners.

In truth, Jerry didn't help much—he mainly provided conversation and poked around, sticking his fingers in this or that to test out the quality of my cooking—but his company was very welcome all the same. Morna, on the other hand, was taking Anne's wish to have an "authentic" feast to heart and was teaching me how to prepare dishes our guests would find familiar.

I was fascinated by everything I was learning. It was ridiculously hard work, but resulted in much simpler, less extravagant dishes in terms of ingredients and techniques. After my first day in the kitchen with Morna, however, I found that simpler didn't mean bland by any stretch of the imagination. I felt much like I had when first attending culinary school, with each new bit of information a revelation that would forever change my cooking. I truly couldn't believe how great things could taste when prepared without modern tools. All that was required was nature, a bit of fire, elbow grease, fresh herbs and seasonings, and patience. The aromas drifting through the kitchen assured me it would be a feast to please everyone, regardless of from which century they came.

With only a few hours remaining until what was now being termed by Anne as "Scotland's take on a ball," and at Morna's insistence that she had everything under control in the kitchen, I left to go change into the stunning period gown Gillian had delivered to my room that morning.

I couldn't wait for the festivities to begin.

Callum looked on with horrified amusement as his clansmen and neighboring lairds piled into the castle. Never for a single moment would he have ever considered hosting such a spectacle on his own. To see the men of his century dressed in their traditional garb, walk through the castle's main doors with their wives and children was a wonder, to be sure. They gawked in awe at every little thing.

"Morna, I look like a wrinkled fool," Jerry grumbled from where he stood with his wife behind Callum. "Even with the shirt, ye can see my legs. No one but ye has seen my legs in near twenty years. Let me go and change. Anne and Gillian willna mind. I beg ye."

Callum smiled even before he turned in Jerry's direction. Of course his old friend would try to squirm out of tonight. Callum would expect nothing less.

Morna scowled at her husband. "Jerry, what are ye talking about? Ye look verra striking in yer kilt. The lassies willna leave ye alone. It makes me feel young just looking at ye."

Callum clasped Jerry on the shoulder. "Ye look quite handsome, Jerry. I'm sure Morna is right. Ye needn't change."

Morna smiled at him in thanks. "That's what I've been telling him, but he's acting like an old man. I've never thought of him as such."

"I'm tired, Morna." Jerry's shoulders slumped. "I doona feel well."

Morna waved a hand in the air dramatically. "Ye shall feel ill in bed, as well. Ye might as well feel ill at the party. I'll not hear another word about it. Now, stand here and speak with Callum or come and help me in the kitchen, but doona ye dare retire to our room."

Callum waited until Morna was gone to shrug at his friend. "My apologies, but I doona think ye've any hope of changing Morna's mind on the matter. If she says ye must enjoy the party, then ye must."

He expected Jerry to argue. It worried him when the old man reached out to lean against the wall for balance instead. "I'd love to enjoy it, lad. I've not seen my wife dressed in such a manner in ages. But I meant what I told her. I doona feel well. Not at all. I need to lie down before I fall down."

Callum moved to support Jerry immediately, glancing to make sure no one could see as he hurried him to the back staircase so he could lead him up to his room. He could tell by Jerry's face how bad he felt, and he knew the old man well enough to be certain that Jerry would not disappoint his wife unless he had no other choice.

It didn't take long to get Jerry settled in bed, and within moments, his eyes began to flutter shut.

"Are ye all right?" Callum asked with concern. "Let me go get Morna, Jerry."

"I'm fine. I just need to rest. Wait until the festivities begin to tell Morna where I am."

Callum nodded but made haste to the kitchen in search of

Morna. Jerry looked very ill; he didn't think it wise to wait until the feast began to let Morna know. Perhaps there was some way she could help her husband.

The only person inside the kitchen was Sydney. Even turned away from him, her beauty took him aback. Her hair was pinned to one side, a long sweeping trail of black he desperately wanted to bury his face in as he wrapped his arms around her.

"Callum. Is everything okay? You look...you look weird."

He swallowed and gathered his thoughts before speaking. "Aye. Do ye know where Morna is? I need to speak with her."

"She's gone to light candles around the dining tables upstairs. You're better off just waiting for her here. I'm sure she's running all over the place right now, but she'll be back in just a few minutes."

"Aye, fine. I'll wait for her. Can I help ye with anything?"

From what he could see, there was nothing else to help with—all of the food was already in the dining hall. He wondered if Sydney stayed down here because it was where she felt the most comfortable.

"No," she assured him, "everything's finished. I just...I wasn't really sure where to go once I was dressed. I didn't want to be in the way." Her gaze swept over him. "You look very nice, Callum."

He felt like a troll standing next to her, but if she thought him handsome, he'd take the compliment any day. "Thank ye. Ye're stunning, Sydney. Ye'll put the rest of the lassies to shame."

She made a dismissive noise and stepped away from him to fiddle with something on the kitchen island. "No, I won't. I would kill for the head of hair Gillian has or for Anne's eyes, but it's certainly kind of you to say so. I think I clean up okay."

"More than that, Sydney. I can scarcely breathe looking at ye." He hoped his admission wasn't too forward. When she smiled, some of his tension released, and he let out the breath he'd not known he held.

"That's kind of you to say."

He smiled back at her. "I'm glad ye dinna take the potion, lass."

She stopped her piddling around and moved over to him, lacing her fingers into his. "I am, too. Do you plan on dancing tonight, Callum?"

"Aye. I'm quite good at it."

She nodded. Both their chests seemed to be rising and falling more quickly than normal as their conversation progressed. "Hmm...I'm sure you are. You'll dance with many girls, then?"

It was a ridiculous question, and he knew she meant to tease him. Surely she knew who he wanted to dance with tonight after the last words he'd said to her. "I may dance with many, but none will capture me the way ye have."

Her smile widened as she stood on the tips of her toes to quickly kiss the end of his nose. "Good. I'm sure glad you didn't expect me to just dance with you. I was looking forward to making my way around the dance floor."

"I take it back, lass. I'll only dance with ye if it means I can keep ye all to myself. I know my men too well. It wouldna please me at all to see ye dancing with another."

Sydney stepped away from him, dismissing his concern. "I can handle myself when it comes to men. Let's just both enjoy the dancing as much as we can."

"Aye, go and have yerself a bonny time, then. I'll find Morna and meet ye later on. I can hear noise stirring above. It seems the feast is starting."

CHAPTER 21

The entire evening had me feeling like an alien on a strange planet. Everything from the utensils used for the feast to the style of dancing in the main hall was unfamiliar. I couldn't seem to keep up with any of it.

It took me a good ten minutes after Callum left me standing in the kitchen to gain control over my breathing again. The effect we seemed to have on one another baffled me. How could I already feel so strongly about someone I scarcely knew at all? If my gut was right, Callum's feelings were a fair match for my own. That possibility both terrified and delighted me.

Callum's good looks had struck me the moment I first saw him, but it truthfully never occurred to me that he would be attracted to me too. In my experience with men, they never were. Not that I believed men found me completely unappealing. But somehow over the years, I'd done a fine job of choosing men to date that I didn't really care for, and an even better job of dating men that cared for me even less.

For a long while, I couldn't see the pattern, but after a string of breakups that left me feeling relieved rather than saddened, I suddenly knew why I always set myself up to fail with men. To nurture mutual feelings in a relationship would require that I put in time and effort, and my job had left me with little to give to anyone.

Perhaps if I'd known how it could make me feel—the heart-pounding, blood-pulsing breathlessness, the anticipation, anxiety, and longing—I would've cared more about what I'd given up for so long.

Now, as I stood weak in the knees and shaky, leaning against one of the walls in the main hall while watching dozens of happy men and women dancing, I couldn't imagine ever again denying myself the possibility of feeling so alive.

I could tell that whatever Callum needed to speak with Morna about was important, so I didn't mind attending the festivities alone until he returned. Crowds, even rowdy ones such as this, didn't make me uncomfortable. I enjoyed meeting new people and conversing with strangers. It was only when the dancing really began and invitations began to come my way that I hesitated. I was nervous about my inability to follow someone's lead.

At first I considered waiting for Callum, but there was no way to know just how long he would be. After a few invitations, I decided that it really didn't matter if I sucked at dancing. I happily took the hand of the stranger standing in front of me as we danced our way back into the center of the crowd.

I quickly realized that my lack of experience with Scottish dancing didn't matter one bit. Each new partner seemed more skilled than the last and led me effortlessly. I glided across the floor, moving easily to another strapping Scot with each new song. I became so swept up in the fun and endless movement that I didn't notice Callum's arrival until his hand reached for my wrist. His swift tug pulled me away from my current partner and spun me into his arms where he smoothly picked up the dance where the last man left off.

I smiled, chiding him as I glanced over my shoulder to see the crestfallen expression on the stranger's face. "You could've let him finish the dance with me."

"No. I couldna wait another moment."

He held me close, much closer than any other partner had. I felt the tightness of his body against me, and it was enough to make me shiver as we spun together.

"Have you been waiting long?" I asked.

"Long enough to see ye dance with three of my cousins and the stable boy. I dinna care for it."

I laughed, secretly tickled by his jealousy. "Well, I did. I was having a great time."

He shrugged his shoulders, and as I glanced up, I noticed that with each new turn, he moved us further away from the crowd.

"Mayhap so, but ye will enjoy dancing with me more. Come . . . We'll still be able to hear the music, but we can dance in private. Ye are not verra good at it. I'd like to spare ye the embarrassment."

"Ha." I laughed, and as he let me go, I crossed my arms indignantly. "No one else seemed to mind what a bad dancer I am."

He smiled and gave me a brief wink. "I doona mind either. 'Twas just an excuse to get ye alone." He jerked his head toward the stairs. "Have ye seen the tower in this time yet?"

To my surprise, I realized I had not. "No, but I'd like to."

"Good."

He took the steps more quickly than I could in my dress, but when we reached the top I decided the climb had been worth the effort. The moon shone brightly through a series of windows surrounding the circular room. Electric torches hung between each pane of glass. Stone benches sat around the outer rim of the space, and the soft sound of music gently reverberated off the stones in a way that made it sound even more beautiful than it had downstairs.

"Wow." It was a fairly pathetic response, but Callum seemed

to appreciate it, mimicking my speech as he smiled and moved to sit on one of the benches, motioning for me to do the same.

"Aye. Wow."

The word sounded funny coming out of his mouth, and I laughed at him as I joined him on the bench. "It looks so much better up here now."

"Aye, but it will look just as beautiful as this in my own time soon."

I knew that was true. Even crumbling, the tower was beautiful. Once whole, it would be as astonishing as it was now.

Noticing a cot on the other side of the room, I asked, "What is that?"

He looked down, and something near embarrassment crossed his face.

"Ach, I meant to put it away before I brought ye here. The tower serves as my bedchamber now—only until the castle is finished."

"Why aren't you in a room?"

"I was for a long while."

"Well, who kicked you out?"

He just grinned back at me, and I realized what I should've from the moment I arrived. Of course there wasn't a spare room for me with as many people as there were currently staying at the castle.

"Oh my gosh. It's me. I kicked you out. You gave up your room so I could stay there. Let's switch. You're the one working so hard. I really don't want to be responsible for putting you out of your room."

He reached up to brush hair from my face, the touch of his thumb trailing its way across my cheek and causing my breath to catch. "I'll not be trading with ye," he said softly. "I'm happy where I am."

"Well, I'm not happy where I am—not now that I know my arrival kicked you out of your room."

He shook his head in frustration. I realized then that my response was exactly why he'd wished to rid the tower of the cot before I could see it.

"Sydney, I willna listen to another word about this. I brought ye here so I could kiss ye senseless, not so ye would worry over where I lay my head at night. Can ye not see the view I have? I go to sleep each night watching the stars above me, all while being warmed by the nearby heater and sleeping on a bed softer than any I've slept on in my life before this time. I'm not suffering, I assure ye."

"All right. I'll let it go." I paused, then asked, "What's that other thing you just said?"

"I doona know what ye mean. That I go to sleep watching the stars?"

I leaned forward to kiss him quickly as a reminder. "No. Not that part. I'm pretty sure you know what I'm referring to."

"Oh, the kissing ye senseless part? Aye, I remember it well."

Our lips met only briefly when a voice interrupted us. "Laird MacChristy! Come quick. We've captured a man many believe to be Macaslan."

The panicked request reached us before the speaker appeared, but by the time the man made it to the tower, Callum was already on his feet and ready to go.

"Are ye certain, lad?" he asked.

"No, sir. I've never seen the man, but others recognized him."

Callum didn't turn toward me as he spoke, but grabbed my wrist so that I would follow him as he hurried down the stairs.

"Sydney, if it is indeed Laird Macaslan, many months of searching and waiting for the monster to make himself known will come to an end this night. Go to yer bedchamber and doona leave until I come and tell ye 'tis safe to do so. Macaslan wouldna come alone. Lock yer door and swear to me ye willna come out. Do ye swear it, lass?"

"Yes, I swear it. Go. I'll be fine. It's not far to my room."

On hearing my words, he released my arm and ran ahead of me.

I'd nearly reached my room when a cold breeze from the open door across from my own drew my attention. Every other door in the hallway was closed. I couldn't resist peeking inside.

The only source of light within came from a few candles burning on the bedside table and the moonlight streaming in from an open window. The room was bright enough that I could clearly see Jerry tucked into his bed, his head propped up on a pile of pillows. With his face turned away from me, he appeared to gaze toward the open window.

I took a step inside, wondering if perhaps a breeze had blown the window open, and Jerry was either too tired or too frail to get up and close it himself.

"Are you cold, Jerry?"

At the sound of my voice, his head whipped toward me. His eyes were wide, and tears streamed down his face.

I rushed toward him. "Is everything all right? Let me close the window for you."

His arm shot out from beneath the covers, and he grabbed my hand, preventing me from going to the window.

"Jerry? What's wrong?" I asked, as he turned away from me again.

Only then did I notice the cloaked figure standing just outside of the moonlight. I'd only heard mention of her once, but I knew immediately who she was.

"Go, Grier," Jerry sobbed, sounding desperate. "Ye must leave here now."

At his words, she stepped into the light and looked directly at him, her expression as pained as his. Tears also streamed down her face. I knew nothing about her other than what Callum had told me, but there was no doubting the intimacy between this woman and Jerry. It was as clear as day in both of their eyes.

"Take what I gave ye, Jerry. 'Tis the only way ye will survive what's stirring within ye."

Jerry released my hand as the witch jumped through the window. I ran to look out, but there was no trace of her. With trembling hands, I closed the window and returned to Jerry's bedside, no longer caring if Macaslan had men roaming about the castle. Jerry's pain seemed so much more pressing than my own safety.

"Why are you crying, Jerry?" I asked.

"A lifetime ago, I made peace with the fact that I would never see Grier again. Even after learning she was alive, I never dreamt our paths would cross. Now that they have, to have her part from me feels like the first time all over again."

"You were close?"

Even if he hadn't responded, his eyes would've been answer enough. "Aye. My memories of her are not as harsh as my wife's. Though I know Morna has good reason for the way she feels about Grier, I doona share her hatred of the lass. Morna owns my heart and always has, but Grier knows my soul in a way no one else ever will."

"And you know hers just as well?"

He reached for my hand again. This time there was less urgency in his squeeze. I brushed the tears from his cheeks with my free hand.

"I do know her soul," he said softly. "She is not the woman Morna believes her to be. Morna will come to see that in time. Grier and I have made a plan."

"A plan?" I smiled at him. The sudden look of excitement on his face made him look like a young, adventurous child rather than the old man he was.

"Aye." He gave a short laugh, but his smile quickly faded as his hand flew to his chest. His face blanched, and he groaned in agony as I stood there, startled and confused.

Struggling to speak, he said, "Doona panic, lass, but I believe I'm having a heart attack. I've aspirin in my bag. Can ye grab it?"

I ran toward his bag, fumbling through it until my hands found the bottle of pills. I opened it as quickly as I could and all but shoved the pills down his throat. As he swallowed, I remembered Grier's words to him before she jumped.

If Jerry believed her harmless, so did I. From the way Callum spoke of the witch, he had the same impression of her. Jerry needed to take whatever she'd left him.

"What did Grier give you? Where is it?" I asked.

He shook his head as he continued to clutch his chest, then rolled over to his side in the bed. I feared he was about to vomit.

"No. I willna take it. If I do so now, Morna will believe that Grier caused this rather than helping it."

I glanced back and forth across the room, looking for anything potion-like in appearance. When I spotted the bottle next to him on the bed, I dove for it.

"I don't care what Morna thinks. Would you rather her find you dead or be suspicious of Grier? We can explain it to her later. Open your stubborn mouth."

His eyes rolled back in his head as he lost consciousness. In the same instant, I pried his mouth open, popped the cork from the bottle, and poured the contents down his throat. Once every last drop was gone, I screamed at the top of my lungs for help.

CHAPTER 22

Cars, as much as Callum loved them, were no longer the most fascinating thing he'd seen during his time in the twenty-first century—not after seeing a hospital. The people there worked on Jerry so quickly, so urgently, that Callum could scarcely believe how things progressed once they arrived.

According to his doctors, Jerry was lucky. The heart attack was mild, and no surgery would be necessary, although he would have to take medication to keep it from happening again. While Jerry was determined to ignore the last piece of the doctor's advice, Callum was determined to make sure he kept it. Lifestyle changes would be a necessity.

"Can ye hurry it along, Callum? I'm ready to be back at the castle. Three days in the hospital is long enough."

Callum continued to drive at the same speed, although he doubted there was any way that Jerry was more eager to arrive than he was. Jerry had been needlessly difficult the entire ride.

"I know ye're ready, but ye'll have to wait a few minutes more."

"I doona know why ye felt the need to stay and care for me.

Ye've got yer own things that need tending to. I would have been fine on my own."

Callum wouldn't dream of leaving his dear friend at the hospital alone to deal with Morna's endless berating. As difficult as Jerry had been over the past days, Morna had been doubly so.

He thought back to the party. After he left the tower to go after Macaslan, he soon realized the lad who'd interrupted him and Sydney had lied. Rather than lead Callum straight to where his enemy was supposedly being held, the messenger had weaved his way through the castle, pretending to be lost. Callum's men had spent so much time in the castle over the past month, he knew not a one of them could ever get lost within Cagair's halls, no matter the century.

It took only a few questions for the boy to come clean. No one had seen Macaslan. There was no one held captive by Callum's men. Instead, a woman the boy didn't know had offered him money to serve as a distraction.

Callum knew the woman must've been Grier. While on his way to search for the witch, he had heard Sydney's screams for help.

Coming back to the present, Callum said to Jerry, "I've nothing that needs tending to, save ye, my friend. Ye needed me there to combat Morna's wishes that she take ye straight from the hospital back home. She is not pleased that we are returning ye to Cagair Castle."

"Aye, I know she isna, but she canna care for me alone, not without her magic, and she's already sworn that she willna use it on me. It will be better that I stay at Cagair until I am better. Her reasons for wanting me away from the castle are not valid. Grier dinna do this to me. I know it, but Morna willna listen."

Callum knew the truth of it too. Morna was just too stubborn and worried about Jerry to accept it.

I knew Jerry was back from the hospital by the extra car parked in front of the castle, but I'd yet to gather the courage to check in on him. The last thing I wanted to do was intrude or be in the way. From everything I'd heard, he would be okay. I couldn't be more thankful for that. If I was ever given the opportunity to see Grier again, I would make certain I hugged her neck.

Once Jerry left for the hospital, my nerves were so shot that I retired to bed straight away. While I heard the party continue on for hours into the night, I couldn't believe how little sign of it there was the next morning. Not only was every guest gone, but every other piece of evidence of the gathering had disappeared as well. The food was put away, dishes cleaned, decorations gone, mess tidied. It astonished me.

When I went to ask Anne how they'd managed it all, she insisted she'd been unable to sleep a wink so she busied herself all night. I immediately felt guilty for not lending a hand, but she assured me that she didn't mind in the slightest.

As I approached the kitchen the morning of Jerry's return, I heard Morna's voice inside and joined her, eager to hear news of Jerry's health. Rather than speaking of her husband, she was lamenting with Anne over Jerry's new diet and her lack of knowledge about healthy foods.

"I doona know what I shall do," Morna complained. "The doctor gave me such little guidance but so much pressure to make changes for him that I fear I may cave under it. He made me feel it's my responsibility. Mayhap it is."

Anne stood with one arm draped around Morna's shoulders, as the older woman sniffled and looked down at the floor. I walked over to them and pulled Morna into a hug.

"What's this?" I asked. "I thought Jerry was doing better. Surely they wouldn't let him leave if he wasn't."

She looked up at me and moved to wipe her hand across her

nose as she took a shaky breath. "Aye. He couldna be more fortunate. 'Tis not often that modern medicine can overcome the powers of a witch's curse. I doona know why I'm so weepy."

I wanted to speak up in defense of Grier, but I didn't think it best with Morna being so upset.

Anne reached over and squeezed my arm to get my attention. "I bet Sydney can help," she told Morna. "She knows everything about food, even healthy food. Don't you, Sydney?"

"Yes. And, of course, I will help. What can I do?"

Morna stepped away to grab a piece of paper off the island. Extending it toward me, she said, "Here are the doctor's guidelines for Jerry's new diet. No salt, no sugar, no dairy, no red meat, no sausage, no bread...the list goes on and on. How am I expected to cook anything at all, let alone something that Jerry will eat? Why, the old man has lived off of salty cheese and sausage most of his life. He ran a farm, but he's not a goat. He canna live by munching on grass alone."

I could see how such restrictions would overwhelm Morna, especially when she was already so shaken by all that had happened over the past few days. But the diet was entirely feasible. It was an opportunity for me to take charge, and I was an expert at that.

"You don't need to worry about any of this, Morna," I told her. "I'll cook everything for him myself until he's much better. In fact, I'll just make sure we are all eating this diet. It will make it easier for Jerry and will be healthier for all of us, besides. And, I'll make sure to draw you up a manageable eating plan, complete with recipes and shopping lists that you can use on your own once you and Jerry return home. You're a good cook, so you won't need help once you have the recipes. You just need some guidance."

The woman's lip trembled in what I could only assume was gratitude. I was thankful she was able to hold herself together. Otherwise, I knew I would be blubbering right along with her.

"Aye, exactly." Morna sniffed. "All I need is some guidance. I canna thank ye enough, Sydney."

"You don't need to thank me at all. It's my job."

I pulled away from the group hug and went to open the refrigerator to look inside. There had been so many leftovers after the party that I had not cooked in days. There was very little in the pantry or fridge.

"May I borrow a car so that I can go get groceries?" I asked. "I don't think there's a thing here that Jerry should eat. It will take me awhile to gather up a proper list, though."

"Of course," said Anne.

"What time is it?" I asked. My stomach was growling in spite of the hearty breakfast I'd eaten earlier. I guessed that Jerry probably hadn't eaten anything all day.

"'Tis near noon," said Morna. "Honestly, lass, I can bake Jerry a piece of chicken if naught else for lunch. There's no need to make Callum wait any longer."

"Actually..." Anne's face twisted up guiltily as she bobbed her head in the direction of the fridge. "I'm pretty sure we're out of chicken. The party went through most of the food, then Orick and Aiden ate the remainder of the meat this morning. All we have is frozen pizza."

Pizza was the very last thing Jerry needed, and it would take me the rest of the day to come up with a proper meal plan and drive to get the groceries.

I shook my head. "Well, Jerry's not eating pizza, and he'll need something before I'm able to get back from shopping. There's a head of lettuce and a few tomatoes in here. I can prepare a salad, but that's not enough to sustain him." As thin as he was, from what I'd seen, Jerry was a healthy eater.

It only took me a moment to recall the small chicken coop I'd noticed next to the stables. It wouldn't be pleasant, but as far out as Cagair was, I didn't see any other option.

I looked at Anne. "Question—the chickens out back—is anyone overly fond of them?"

Her face blanched as she widened her eyes and shook her head at me. "No, I don't think so. You're not going to...to kill one, are you?"

"I certainly am. How do you think the chicken you buy at the store gets there? Somebody has to kill it. I've never done it before, but I remember watching my grandmother do it. I'll manage."

I walked out of the kitchen rather determinedly, hoping that I would be able to finish the unpleasant task before I talked myself out of it.

CHAPTER 23

No one could say that I wasn't the sort of person to do what I said I was going to. Killing it may have caused me to retch twice, but I had a perfectly cooked, appropriately seasoned chicken breast delivered to Jerry's room within the hour. The real casualty out of the whole ordeal seemed to be Anne. I didn't know if I turned her into a vegetarian, or if she was just frightened I might ask her for help cooking one day, but she disappeared for hours.

Today, however, I really didn't care either way. I pushed through it, but the act was just as traumatizing for me as it was for Anne. When I finished cooking, I escaped to my room to shower the icky feeling away.

It was mid-afternoon by the time I emerged from my room with the intent to check on Jerry and find Callum. It was silly, I knew, but three days away from him seemed like a very long time. I hoped he was as anxious to see me as I was to see him.

I was still without groceries for the rest of the week, but thankfully, Aiden agreed to go shopping first thing in the morning to spare me the trip today if I would give him a list at dinner.

I learned from Cooper that Callum had spent the majority of the day at Jerry's side, so I crossed the hall to Jerry's room, hoping to find them both inside. With that in mind, I stood outside his bedroom and knocked loudly, lifting my free palm up to my mouth to gently test out my breath. I'd brushed and swished mouthwash twice, but I wanted to be certain that all traces of vomit were now gone.

When no response came, I called out while knocking even more loudly a second time. "Jerry, are you awake?"

I realized how thoughtless my question was the moment I asked it. If he wasn't awake before, he certainly was now.

"Aye, I'm awake. Come and join us," came his reply.

I pushed open the door slightly and hesitantly stepped inside. Callum sat next to Jerry's bed. He twisted and grinned at me as I entered.

Jerry continued to beckon me forward. "Come here, lass. I've missed ye."

It seemed funny to me that he'd miss me after our few interactions together, but I felt much the same, and it lifted my mood greatly to see him so chipper.

I placed my hand on Callum's shoulder in greeting before leaning in to kiss Jerry on the cheek. "You look good, Jerry," I said. Just the touch of my hand on Callum's shoulder made my stomach flutter. I ignored the sensation and focused on Jerry. "How are you feeling?"

"Much better than I was. It seems I need to thank ye twice over, first for not letting me die, and second for cooking me such a delicious piece of chicken. I've never had poultry that tasted so fresh."

At mention of his lunch, my stomach surged for an entirely different reason than it had just seconds before. "Well, yes, it definitely was fresh."

"What does that mean, lass?" Jerry chuckled slightly as he

asked the question, and I knew by the ornery glint in his eye that he already knew the answer.

"Morna told you, didn't she?"

"Aye. They've one less chicken in the coop from what I hear."

Callum twisted to look at me with a shocked expression. "No, ye dinna? I doona believe it."

"I did, but I really don't want to talk about it. I do, however, wish to speak with you. Will you come with me?"

"Aye." Callum started to stand.

Jerry reached out a hand to prevent us from leaving. "No, please doona leave. I'm bored to tears in this bed. I'm verra good at acting like it's always Morna intruding into other people's business, but I'm rather nosy myself. Just go ahead and have yer conversation and allow me to lay back and listen."

Even his sly smile wouldn't convince me to do what I wished to in front of Jerry. "I know you must be losing your mind, but this is rather personal. It's not even a conversation, really. There's something—"

Callum interrupted me before I could continue. "Oh come, Sydney. Jerry's good at keeping secrets. What do ye need to say? I've no problem hearing it in front of Jerry if it will make him happy. He's a trying fool when he's not in good mood."

I suddenly viewed the situation much like the one with the chicken. If I didn't just do it, I would talk myself out of it. I didn't want to talk myself out of it—I'd wanted to kiss Callum again for days now.

"Fine." I bent to grab Callum's face with both hands, lifting his head upward so I could kiss him. It was a very good kiss. When I pulled away, both men stared at me with expressions that I guessed resembled Anne's as she watched me murder the chicken. It seemed I was on a roll with the unexpected today.

"Now, can we speak alone?" I asked.

Callum didn't wait for Jerry's permission as he stood and

latched onto my hand, pulling me out of the room behind him. "I'm sorry, Jerry," he called back over his shoulder. "I'll not be saying no to her, not if there's a chance she may do that again."

"O'course, lad. Get out of here, the both of ye." He chuckled. "The lass made my month with that."

CHAPTER 24

Three days was no time at all in the grand scheme of things, but three days spent doing very little other than thinking was a very long time indeed. While I used my kiss as a way to draw Callum's attention away from Jerry's bedside, it was certainly not the only reason I wanted him alone. While Callum and Jerry were away, I had developed a long list of things I wanted to talk over with him.

Jerry's heart attack frightened everyone, and the event made it plain to me that it didn't matter that I'd yet to mark a week here at Cagair. I cared about these people. I felt comfortable around them. And despite the hiccup of my first night here, I trusted them completely.

As far as I could see, time wasn't necessarily the best marker for change. Life could change in an instant—the past week was evidence of that. Or, as my entire time in Italy demonstrated, years could go by with nothing of interest ever happening. I trusted my feelings enough not to worry about the timeline in which they progressed.

I could deal with that, but what if Callum couldn't? What if days away from me had cooled his feelings? Even if they hadn't cooled, what exactly *were* his feelings for me, anyway? His promise to pursue me certainly got my blood pumping, but I needed clarity on what we were doing.

Even if he technically lived in another century, the portal made it too easy for him to travel back and forth. We would bump into each other all the time, even once the repairs on his castle were finished. I already enjoyed my new job immensely, and I suspected that my love for it would continue to grow over time. I had every intention, Callum aside, to be at Cagair long-term. So would he. I didn't believe our feelings for one another could be pursued casually with no thought about the possible ramifications later.

What if things got messy and didn't work out? I didn't want that to impact my job here, or worse, to affect my relationships with the rest of the household. All of it needed to be talked through.

"Hang on." My plea came out breathlessly as he nipped gently at my neck, holding me close with one hand as he swung the door to my bedroom shut with the other. If I didn't get the conversation going soon, my desire to talk would melt away from the warmth of his touch. "Callum, I want to talk to you."

He paused with his lips still touching my neck, holding his stance for just a moment before stepping back. "Oh. Ye truly wish to speak? With the way ye acted in front of Jerry, I thought perhaps this is what ye meant by talking."

He couldn't look more disappointed.

"I meant both sorts of talking, but if we proceed with this kind first, the other will never happen."

He grinned and nodded as he led me over to the edge of the bed.

"Aye, 'tis true. What do ye wish to speak of?"

"You don't really know me—not well, not yet—but you'll find soon enough that I tend to be very blunt. I've never seen much sense in beating around the bush about anything."

He nodded, urging me onward. "I agree, lass. Say what ye need to."

"Okay, right. Well, firstly, I think maybe I need some clarification on exactly what we are doing, because if you answer one way, the rest of what's on my mind will be moot."

"Aye, I've some pressure then."

He appeared calm, but for someone who'd just claimed that I didn't like to beat around the bush, I certainly seemed to be stalling. It had to be making him nervous.

"No. No pressure. Just answer honestly. You've only known me a few days, so whatever you say will be fine." I took a breath. "When you said the other day that you were going to pursue me ardently, did that mean you are interested in a relationship of sorts, or only a . . . well, a hookup?"

He crossed his arms and regarded me cautiously. Chuckling slightly, he said, "If by hookup ye mean what I think ye do, doona tell me that either answer is fine, for I doona know of any lass who would care for that answer, but I will answer ye truthfully all the same."

He uncrossed his arms and reached for my hand, bringing it up to his mouth so that he could kiss the inside of my palm. "I am not the sort of man who easily separates the urgings of my body from the urgings of my heart. The two are closely tied and always have been. Ye can be assured that I wish to get to know yer mind and heart, Sydney. Though ye are lovely, it is not just yer looks that interest me."

"Good. I feel the same way." Relieved, I continued, "Now, you should know before we continue that I'm not like a lot of people when it comes to dating. I'm too work-driven, too independent. There must be some boundaries, okay?"

He laughed and leaned in to kiss my cheek. "What do ye mean by boundaries?"

"I mean that I make my own decisions. Don't ever, even for a second, think that you can tell me what to do and I will listen. In fact, the fastest way to get me to do something is to tell me not to. As childish as that may be, it's just the truth."

His brows lifted.

I didn't wait for him to respond before jumping into the most pressing matter on my mind. "One last thing—what if this doesn't work? Will you be able to peacefully coexist so that it doesn't impact my job here? I'm already so fond of everyone. I would hate it if weirdness between us made it uncomfortable for everyone else. I know I can manage to separate everything. Can you?"

He shook his head, and something within me deflated. "Truthfully, I doona know. I feel I'm already too fond of ye to see such an occasion arising."

"Yeah, but it might."

He stood, smiled, and extended a hand to pull me to my feet. "I truly doona think it will. Even if it does, mayhap it's not the best idea to go into anything expecting it to fail, aye?"

Callum pulled me closer and bent to kiss me, and I decided that perhaps I was approaching everything far too pessimistically.

He whispered in my ear before kissing the side of my neck. "Now, let's get about the business of speaking another way, if ye doona mind. I've been waiting to kiss ye again for far too long."

I surrendered to his kiss, happily losing myself in it. He kissed me so deeply that all worry drifted from my mind. For now, I decided, I would gladly stay lost in his touch. As long as I stayed cautious and kept a gauge on the pace of things, there was no harm in our enjoyment of being together.

CHAPTER 25

650

Callum stood on the makeshift ladder, spreading the mortar for the stones. He worked alongside Taran, the best mason in all of Scotland. The work required a great deal of attention, and Callum didn't want to stop for a short respite midday with the rest of his men.

"What?" Callum scowled down at his brother, Adwen, who waited at the foot of the ladder with Orick. "Can ye wait a while longer? Why doona the two of ye come up here if ye wish to talk to me?"

"No. Get yerself down here."

The sound of Adwen's voice told Callum his brother was giving him an order, not a choice.

"We've already waited a good deal of time for ye," Adwen continued. "Taran doesna need ye. Ye are more likely in his way than ye are help to him."

Callum cast a questioning glance in Taran's direction. The old man laughed as he answered, "I wouldna say that ye are in my way, but Adwen is right; I'll be just fine on my own. Go and see what he wants so he will quit hollering."

Handing the tools over, Callum wiped his palms clean and descended the tower. When he reached the bottom, he was near ready to punch his brother square in the nose. "What is the matter with ye? Nora has more patience than ye do. What do ye want?"

Adwen didn't answer as he started off.

Orick clasped Callum on the shoulder as they made their way outside of the castle together. "We need ye to settle a wager between us," Orick said. "Ye'd think he would've learned his lesson after what Griffith did to him the last time with a bet. But I suppose Adwen needs one more loss before sense finds him."

Callum expected that, whatever their wager, Adwen would lose; he always did. "What is yer wager? I canna see how I can settle it."

Orick winced. "Now, before I tell ye, allow me to remind ye that 'twas not I that came up with the wager. Adwen is the scoundrel, not I. 'Tis only that I derive much pleasure from seeing Adwen change Nora's diapers for a month. That is the only reason I bet him."

Shaking his head, Callum sighed impatiently. "Get on with it. What did ye wager?"

Adwen stepped suddenly between them, apparently fed up with waiting on Orick to explain. "I told him that ye've already made a fool of yerself over Sydney. Orick disagrees."

"Aye, I disagree." Orick shoved Adwen out of the way.

Callum thought how childish they seemed in that moment. "Made a fool of myself in what way?"

"The wager is," Adwen said with a smirk, "that she's already slapped yer face at least once.

Orick made a scoffing sound. "I told him that ye are not the same hasty fool that he is, that ye take a little more care with yer women. I was right, aye? Please tell me ye are not the cad yer brother thinks ye to be."

Callum turned away from them and proceeded to march back toward the castle. "If either of ye want to know the answer," he called over his shoulder, "ye will have to come with me and help gather up the last batch of stone to haul up to the tower for Taran."

Minutes later, Callum laughed quietly when both men joined him in the storage room. "I knew neither one of ye could bear the suspense." He grinned at them as he hefted a stone. "The truth of the matter is, I've not been slapped by Sydney nor any other lass."

"Damn ye, Orick," Adwen growled. "Why are ye always right about everything?"

Adwen's aggravated voice was enough to make both Callum and Orick burst into pleased laughter.

"Are ye really so surprised, Adwen?" Callum asked. " Doona ye know me better than that?"

Adwen squinted at him. "How do I know yer being honest?"

"Have ye ever known yer brother not to be a man of his word?" Orick asked, with a friendly slap to Adwen's back.

"I guess not." Adwen studied Callum as he worked. "I knew that ye liked her, but... ye care for this lass, doona ye? I hear it in yer voice."

He did care for her—so much so that, for the first time since the repairs on the castle began, he wished he could slow them down.

"Aye, I do care for Sydney," Callum admitted. "I wish to take my time getting to know the lass, though my feelings are progressing more quickly than they should."

Without saying a word about the process, the men formed a line, passing each piece of stone to the other as they worked in tandem to place them inside the wooden wheelbarrow. They would gather up the pieces here then form another tag-team line to haul them up the stairs to the tower.

As they worked, Orick asked, "How do ye mean? 'Tis my own experience that feelings needn't be rushed or stalled. They appear and leave us just as they should—as they are meant to."

Callum took the large rock Orick handed him and turned to pass it off to Adwen. "There is much that needs to be settled before I am ready to share the company of another in my life. The castle restorations need to be finished and the rest of ye seen safely home. I need to see Macaslan dead and buried and Laird Allen repaid for his help and kindness in the search. I've spent too much time away from my territory, from serving the needs of my people. They've spent far too long helping me with my own needs. I should wait until all of these things are accomplished before indulging in the joy Sydney's company brings me, but when I find myself around her, rather than push her away, I urge her to ignore her own misgivings about the speed with which we've come to care for each other. 'Tis selfish and foolish and willna likely end well for either of us."

Adwen laughed, and both Callum and Orick turned to look at him with curious expressions.

Composing himself, Adwen said, "Forgive me for borrowing a phrase from my foul-mouthed wife, but everything ye just said is horse crap."

"Why do ye think that, brother?" Callum asked, trying not to be offended.

"If ye wait until ye are ready, ye'll find us throwing dirt on top of yer dead body before that day comes. No one is ever ready for anything that comes to us in this life. I believe 'twas ye that convinced me not to throw such a gift away when I was in the midst of great grief. I canna see reason for ye to talk yerself out of the possibility of such love for yerself now. Ye are frightened. Why?"

Callum held up a hand to keep Orick from passing him the next stone. Turning to face his brother, he said, "When I sent ye from this castle to go find Jane, I dinna know anything. I'd not experienced love for myself. And aye, I'm frightened. I'm frightened that within a week I'll be so besotted with the lass that I'll scarcely be able to let her go."

Adwen scowled. Sounding frustrated, he said, "Then doona. Why should ye let Sydney go? From the way things appear to me, she doesna intend to leave Cagair. Ye will be but a staircase away from her. If ye wish to move slowly with the lass, fine, but doona deny yerself just because ye are scared. Those in love live in fear always. 'Tis the price we pay."

Orick squeezed his shoulder with a huge, dirty hand. "Adwen is right, Callum."

Eager to hear whatever his friend had to say, Callum turned toward him. Orick was wiser than all of them, and Callum trusted that wisdom.

"If her own feelings do not yet match yer own, it doesna mean that they never shall," Orick proceeded. "Ye doona know what the lass has been through. Mayhap men have not treated her as they should have before. Mayhap she needs to know with certainty how ye feel before her heart will open fully. Reassure her in every sense that ye care. Ye already know that she does. It doesna mean that yer own feelings move too quickly if hers move more slowly."

Callum sighed. "How do ye always know just what everyone needs to hear, Orick?"

Adwen's deep and aggravated voice joined in. "'Tis damned annoying, is it not? The fool knows everything."

Orick hurried to defend himself. "No. I doona know verra much at all, but I do know the two of ye verra well."

"That ye do, Orick." Callum turned to face Adwen. "Ye helped me much this day as well, brother. Fatherhood has changed ye."

Adwen grinned. "The wee babe has stolen my heart, but she has not improved my wisdom. My words to ye today were a stroke of luck. Doona expect such good guidance from me again."

Callum laughed and reached up to grab the men by their

shoulders. "I willna. Still, I appreciate both of ye more than ye know."

Orick shrugged his hand off, dismissing his gratitude just as Callum expected he would. "Ye should know that we appreciate ye as well. All of us do. Ye traveled with yer father for years, even though ye dinna truly wish to; ye took over Cagair Castle so that Adwen could live the life he wished; ye almost married my wife to keep her from Macaslan's wretch of a son. Ye are a selfless man, Callum. If ye've found joy, cling to it with all that ye have."

A sense of urgency swept through Callum. "I will try to, but I canna give her promise of anything until Macaslan is dead."

Adwen gave him a quick slap upside his head. "Callum, ye are trying to talk yerself out of things again. Macaslan has no allies to help him. Even his own men hate him. I'd wager that all danger has passed. I doona think he will return to Scotland ever again."

Chills passed through Callum at his brother's words, intensifying the urgency he felt. If Adwen was willing to bet that all danger had passed, it most certainly had not.

CHAPTER 26

Four Weeks Later—Present Day

Everyone gathered to say goodbye to the Conalls on the morning of their departure from Cagair Castle. They were by far the largest group, and the halls were sure to be quieter without them there. While all seemed pleased that the only things remaining to set Cagair Castle right again were the window coverings and furnishings, a sense of sadness hung over everyone as the first group of guests walked down the stairwell one-by-one.

In the madness of all that had happened over the past weeks, I'd not been able to visit with most of the Conalls as I'd wished to. I was especially disappointed to see Blaire go, however. She still had several months of pregnancy remaining, but she wouldn't feel like traveling anywhere soon. I knew it was wise for the Conalls to leave earlier than the others. Even so, I would miss my brief, daily conversations with Blaire. Her pregnancy cravings had sent her popping in and out of the kitchen quite regularly.

Blaire was the last to travel through, and I smiled as she

waddled over to me for one last farewell. "I canna tell ye how pleased I am ye showed up here," she said, taking my hands in hers. "I'm certain I'll see ye again, for 'tis clear to me ye've fallen for Callum completely. Doona fight it, Sydney. 'Twould be senseless for ye to do so."

I knew it would be pointless for me to argue with her. Despite my initial concerns and hesitations, Callum had thoroughly worn me down over the past few weeks. I accepted the fact that I was very much in love with him. Not that I had told him so. I wouldn't. Not for a very, very long time.

"I'll try not to fight it. I promise," I assured her.

"Even if ye tried, ye willna be able to for long. Believe me, next I see ye, ye will be good and married and caring for Callum's territory at his side."

The thought sent nervous shivers through my stomach. I very much hoped Callum couldn't hear Blaire's predictions for our future together from where he stood. Even though I already loved him, we were still in the early stages of getting to know one another; marriage was surely the very last thing on his mind, as it was mine.

"We'll see," I said with a cautious tone in my voice. "I do hope I see you sooner rather than later, though." I squeezed her hands. "Have safe travels, and please send word when the baby comes."

She hugged me before following the rest of her group into the past.

Once she disappeared, I went in search of my training partner, Cooper.

"*A*re you ready, Cooper?" I asked. "Last I saw Jerry, he was not very excited about the prospect of stair work today. I'm really going to need your help to encourage him."

Cooper ran out of his room and down the hallway the second I finished speaking.

"I was born ready," he said. "It doesn't matter that Jerry doesn't want to do stairs. He has to do them so he can get well enough to tend to his sheep again. He loves those wooly creatures, and I bet they're missing him."

I jogged after the boy, catching him in just a few strides. "I'm sure they are. Let's go drag Jerry out of bed."

When we reached Jerry and Morna's room, Jerry lay with the comforter draped snugly over his head—a sure sign he intended to make our task as difficult as possible. Cooper and I were used to it by now.

The changes in Jerry's diet were, after a few days of unrest, easy enough to implement. While everyone in the castle adhered to the doctor's rules for the two days after Jerry's return from the hospital, it wasn't long before the men and a few of the women began to protest the predominantly vegetarian and lean meat-based diet.

Thank goodness I'd been correct in thinking that all Morna really needed was guidance. As long as I provided her a menu and made sure the groceries were on hand, she had no problem cooking Jerry's food herself. That left me free to prepare more decadent cuisine for the rest of us.

However, the changes in Jerry's exercise routine—or lack thereof—well, that was where the real challenge came in. After taking it upon myself to make certain that he got in at least a little walking and light exercise every day, I quickly realized he was the sort of man that believed life itself should be exercise enough. While that might have been true when Jerry was young and working long, hard days on his farm, he no longer garnered enough "life" activity to cut it.

I attempted the first day of Jerry's rehabilitation solo, but after one temper tantrum from the normally kind old man, I decided I was never going into that room alone again. So...I enlisted Cooper's help. Everyone loved Cooper; I knew Jerry would watch his behavior so much more carefully with the boy present than he did when he and I were alone. I was right. So after his first time assisting me with Jerry's physical therapy, Cooper came along with me every day.

The McMillans planned to remain at Cagair until Jerry was well enough for Morna to take him home, and I couldn't be more thankful for it. If not for Cooper, I expected Jerry would have half the strength he did now.

"Hey, Jerry," Cooper said in his perky little voice when we entered the old man's room. "We're here to get you moving again. Come on sleepy head. Get up out of that bed. You know Sydney —she'll pull you out if you don't get out yourself."

Cooper ran straight toward Jerry's bed, jumped up beside him, and gave him a good shake.

Jerry's grumpy and irritated voice answered, "I'm not sleeping, Cooper, I just doona wish to move about today. Why doona the two of ye just give me one day of rest? I beg ye."

I stepped up to the bed and gave the comforter one quick pull so that it came off the bed entirely. "You can beg all you want, but we aren't going anywhere. Isn't that right, Cooper?"

"Yep," said Cooper, nodding enthusiastically.

"Come on. Get up." I crossed my arms. "You know you're feeling much better. What with all of the good food you are eating and the daily exercise we are making certain you get, you're just glowing with good health. If you can honestly tell me that you've felt better in the last ten years than you do now, I will leave you be."

Jerry uncurled himself and slowly swung his feet over the side of the bed.

"If by *better* ye mean that I have to run to the toilet five times a day just to rid myself of the vegetables Morna keeps shoving down my throat then, aye, I suppose I feel much better."

Cooper laughed until he doubled over. Speaking between

choked, cackling breaths, he gasped, "Well, believe me, Jerry, you'd rather get rid of it than not. If you don't, and my mom finds out, she'll be tempted to stick one of those icky suppose-pi-tory thingies up your backside. Last time she gave me one of those, I was four and a half, and I decided right then that I'd rather not keep holding everything in to keep from suffering that torture again."

Jerry's bad mood vanished in an instant, and the three of us laughed until we hurt all over before taking Jerry out to master his assigned three flights of stairs.

CHAPTER 27

1650

Try as he might, Callum could never convince Tom to stay away from Cagair for even a day. After what he'd been through, Callum wouldn't blame Tom if he refused to step foot on the castle grounds ever again, but the old man had done just the opposite. As soon as he recovered from the injuries he'd sustained on the night of the fire, he returned to his job of checking on the castle on a daily basis.

"Tom, ye needn't have made the trip up here today. Everyone, save the craftsmen, is home enjoying their families. Ye should do the same."

"Ye know I can only bear so much coddling from my wife before I begin to feel ill all over again." Tom's gaze swept over the castle, and his grin spread wide. "It is a happy day. Yer home is now complete, and ye are free to sleep in it this night. I wanted to see it for myself."

With everyone else enjoying a day of relaxation either at home in the village or at the Cagair of the twenty-first century, Callum had been left on his own to enjoy the excitement over the last of the reconstruction. He gladly shared in this moment of joy with Tom. "'Tis a verra happy day, indeed. So many months of labor have finally come to an end."

Tom's grin fell away and he lowered his head, staring at the ground awkwardly.

"What is it, Tom? Yer never shy. I can tell ye are holding something in."

"I shouldna mention it. Not on this day. But I've not had a chance to catch ye alone in some time. Have ye...have ye received word from Laird Allen since he left? Have they had any luck tracking down Macaslan?"

Callum had wondered the same thing as of late. He knew it would take some time for Laird Allen and his men to travel such a great distance. But even if they found nothing, he expected to receive word any day now. "No. Not yet, but I'm sure I will soon. Laird Allen seemed as eager to rid the world of Macaslan as the rest of us, and his men looked a fearsome lot."

As if summoned by their words, the sound of hooves approaching caused both men to turn and look for the rider headed their way.

"Did ye see him on yer way here, Tom?" Callum asked. "Is that why ye mentioned this?"

Tom shook his head. "No, I dinna see a thing. Do ye think 'tis news from Laird Allen?"

"If not from Raudrich, then from one of the others we have stationed about at every port and territory."

"Aye."

The rider looked young—no more than twenty, Callum guessed. He seemed tired, as if he'd ridden through the night to reach them.

Callum took a step forward and called out to the rider. "Greetings. Who has sent ye here?"

The boy pulled hard on his reins to stop the horse, then dismounted. He carried a small leather pouch in his left hand as he approached.

"Lad, I'll ask ye again. Who has sent ye here?" Callum called out.

The boy stopped and took a moment to catch his breath. "Pardon me, sir. It's been a long ride." When his breathing steadied, he continued, "Laird Allen sent me, sir. He asked me to bring ye a gift to celebrate the finishing of yer castle."

The messenger extended the pouch, and Callum accepted it. Lifting the flap, he pulled out an ornate pin—the Macaslan insignia. He recognized it immediately as the one the Laird himself always wore. He knew at once that this was Laird Allen's way of telling him that Macaslan had been killed.

Relieved, Callum handed it to Tom. "Ye've been avenged."

resent Day

he next day, I approached Jerry's room with trepidation. Cooper had come down with a cold that kept him from assisting me today.

At the doorway, I was shocked to see Jerry already dressed and sitting by the fire.

"Well, look at you," I exclaimed, smiling. "How long have you been up?"

He turned and grinned, then pointed to the empty seat across from him. "All day, lass," he said as I headed straight for the chair and sat. "I finally decided there is no sense in feigning that I feel worse than I truly do. Ye and Morna have seen me well."

I knew he was feeling better, but I'd thought he was giving me a hard time about his exercises out of stubborn laziness. It hadn't occurred to me for a second that he'd been trying to pretend he felt bad. I crossed my arms and frowned at him. "Why would you ever feign such a thing?"

"Because I wanted to see Callum's Cagair finished, and I knew that Morna would take me home as quickly as she could if I let her know how well I was feeling. Besides, the plan that Grier and I made would have been too difficult to manage during the castle's repairs. The completion allows us the perfect excuse."

Jerry's mention of said plan before his attack had nagged at me for well over a month. I'd asked him about it countless times, to no avail. Trying again, I said, "Oh, so are you finally ready to tell me about it?"

"Aye, Sydney, I think that I am. Will ye keep the secret?"

"Absolutely."

"I plan to tell Morna that I wish to go down the stairwell—that I wish to see the repaired Cagair myself."

Everyone in the castle knew of Jerry's aversion to all things magic. How he ever managed to entwine himself with not one, but two very powerful witches, I hadn't a clue. For someone whose life was so inundated with sorcery, he was oddly resistant to it all. I knew full well that his insistence that I not give him Grier's potion the night of his attack had just as much to do with his resistance to magic as it had with him fearing Morna's reaction to Grier's part in it.

I frowned at him. "Your wife will never believe that. I've heard you say that you'd never go back."

"Well, I'm not keen on it, to be sure. But I'll overcome my own fears if it means putting to bed all of this between the two of them. And it doesna matter if Morna believes me, lass. All that matters is that she responds as I know she shall."

"How do you think she will respond?"

He laughed and bobbed his head toward the doorway. Morna

was entering the room. "I'll show ye. Watch," he whispered under his breath.

Morna's smile was wider than I'd ever seen it. She didn't seem to see me as she walked over to press a kiss on her husband's lips. "Jerry, I'm so pleased to see ye up and out of that bed. Why, surely that means we can return home soon."

He winked at me over Morna's shoulder. "Aye, but first do ye not wish to go through the stairwell yerself and see the repairs on Cagair before we leave? I willna mind waiting if ye wish for Callum to escort ye through."

"Ha! Ye are a funny man to suggest such a thing, Jerry. Ye know I've no desire to do so."

"Are ye sure, Morna? Ye might enjoy it. Ye wouldna have to stay for more than an hour."

She laughed, and I could see she thought he spoke only in jest. I rather pitied her ignorance in this situation. Jerry was taking great advantage of it.

"I'm completely sure," Morna said firmly. "Ye know what? I'll make ye a deal, Jerry. If ye wish to walk down those steps, I'll be the first to follow ye."

Jerry waved his hand in dismissal of her proposition. "Ach, Morna. Ye know me too well. I'd rather walk over hot coals than do such a thing."

"I know, and I'm glad for it." Morna bent to kiss him once more, then finally greeted me as she turned to leave the room. "I just wanted to stop in and check on him. I best get back and work on his dinner."

Jerry leaned back in his chair as she left, a look of smugness on his face that astonished me completely.

"What was that?" I scowled at him. "You didn't tell her that you planned to go through."

"That was exactly what I knew she would do. And no, I dinna tell her. Not seriously. I'll only do so when I really mean to walk down those steps. She will follow, thinking I'm teasing her once again. Then when I go through, she'll be so shocked that she'll run right after me. When we both get through to the other side, Grier will be waiting."

Propping my elbows on my knees, I leaned forward and pressed my fingertips hard against my forehead. The very thought of the chaos such a plan would cause made my head ache. "That sounds like a really terrible idea, Jerry. Morna seems to have dropped the Grier thing, for whatever reason. Don't you think you're better off leaving well enough alone and going on home and just forget about it?"

His eyes grew wide, as if I'd said something awful. "Lass, if ye think Grier will allow me to go back on my word to her, then I gave ye a kinder impression of her than I intended. She's not the wretch Morna thinks she is, but she's no saint, either. I havena a choice. Besides, I love that it's a terrible idea. 'Tis been far too long since I've done anything foolish."

I stood in the kitchen with my back to the entryway, scrubbing dishes with a little more force than necessary to rid myself of the stress Jerry's words caused me. Suddenly, I felt Callum's arms wrap around me from behind. He rested his chin gently on the top of my head and ran his hands up and down my arms.

"What are you up to?" I asked in a teasing voice, all of my tension melting away.

"The castle is finished, and all of the workers from the village are gone."

I smiled but continued to scrub and rinse the dishes in front of me. "I know. You told me last night this should be the last day of work for them."

"Aye, and it finally is. Will ye stay with me there tonight? I think it would be good luck to have ye there with me my first night back within its walls."

My hands stilled in the warm water, my pulse speeding up significantly. Over the past weeks, we'd grown remarkably close. Our conversations were intimate and our chemistry palpable. But even with as much as we'd kissed and caressed, that had been the extent of our relationship.

I enjoyed our leisurely pace. He'd seemed content with it as well. Not that I wasn't eager to move to the next step; I certainly was. But his question surprised me.

Reaching for the towel spread across the drain tray, I dried my hands but continued to keep my back to him. "I thought you didn't want me going back down the stairwell until Macaslan is caught." As soon as the words were out of my mouth, realization rose within me and I faced him, resting the middle part of my back against the counter. "Was he captured?"

"Macaslan is dead, and I am glad for it. Laird Allen sent a rider who gave me Macaslan's personal insignia that he always wore, along with a message from the rider that he'd been killed."

"You say you're glad, but you don't sound it. Callum, what's wrong?"

"Nothing's wrong. 'Tis only that I canna celebrate killing, deserved or not. 'Tis a serious matter, and I am a traveler, not a warrior. I doona have a thirst for the sort of violence Lord Macaslan endured."

I swallowed. "How was he killed?"

"He was beheaded."

"And you don't approve of that form of . . . um . . . punishment?"

"Aye, I approve. It was a just punishment." He pulled me closer to him. "Let's not talk of it any longer. Ye are safe to visit my world now; that is all that matters."

I nodded. "Let me kiss some color back into your face."

We kissed until we were each breathless and shaky. Then, still embracing, Callum said quietly, "Can I take that as an aye, lass? Ye will travel to my time and stay at the castle there with me this night? With Macaslan dead, I've no reason to fear fer yer safety. 'Twould bring me great happiness to have ye there."

I smiled against his chest. "Yes, I'll travel with you and stay the night. I can't wait to be in your world again. To experience it with you."

———

1 ⁶⁵⁰

Callum couldn't remember ever being so nervous. There was much to celebrate. He had no doubt it would be a glorious night, but he wanted everything perfect before Sydney's arrival.

"Hurry, Jane. It willna take Sydney and Morna long to clean up after the evening meal. Sydney will be expecting me to get her soon."

Jane chunked a pillow at his head and laughed loudly as it hit him square in the nose. "You just need to calm down and take a breath. She's not going to want to get anywhere near you if you keep sweating like that." She walked toward him, gripped both of his arms tightly, and gave him a good shake. "Seriously, what is the matter with you? Why are you so worked up?"

Women didn't understand. They expected greatness of men, to be swept off their feet, to be loved in a way that made them forget the rest of the world, at least for a while. It was all that men wanted to give their women, too, but it was bloody hard work to accomplish such a feat—especially when one was as out of practice, as he was.

"Nothing is the matter, Jane. I'm just verra fond of the lass."

She glared up at him, completely unsatisfied with his answer. "Well, duh. We all know that. Oh..."

Callum cringed inwardly at Jane's quick uptake. She knew the truth without him even saying a word.

"I see. How long has it been, then?" she asked.

He pulled away from her grasp and set about lighting the many candles he had scattered about his room, hoping that if he ignored Jane's question, she would eventually give up and go away. Was he a lovesick fool to prepare his own room in such a way in case Sydney's agreement to spend the night at the castle led them here? He hoped not. But if his hopes were not to be, the guest bedchamber next door had been readied for her as well.

Jane made a huffing sound, pulling him out of his thoughts. "All right, candle boy. For someone who lost their home to a fire not that long ago, you're sure getting a little free and easy with the flames. Cool it. Answer my question."

"Jane." He hung the torch back on the wall and turned toward her, anger rising up in him. "'Tis none of yer business."

"Don't give me that. I was just going to try to give you a pep talk because, clearly, you are in need of one. Never mind. I'll just be on my way. I think I'll be taking this mighty fine, expensive bottle of wine back with me. I'd rather down it myself than gift it over to you at this point." She stomped like a child toward the doorway.

Waiting to speak until she was about to step out in the hallway, Callum said, "Ye are a pain in my backside, Jane MacChristy. Ye and my brother couldna be a better match for one another." He took a breath. "If ye must know, 'tis been two years."

"What?" Her voice reached an unpleasantly high pitch as she whirled on him.

"Ye heard me just fine, Jane."

"Why?"

He ground his teeth together. He wasn't like his brother. He would never be comfortable speaking of such matters. "What do ye mean, *why*? Do ye think 'twas my choice? If ye doona recall, I've been quite busy over the past few years running after my father and brother, always getting them out of trouble. I've not been in seclusion. I've simply been distracted."

Her expression softened as she moved to offer him the bottle of wine. "Yes, you have been. It's high time someone perfect for you came your way. I very much hope your abstinence streak ends this evening." Jane winked at him as he took the bottle from her hands. "You stay and finish up here. I'm going to light the fireplace in the sitting room downstairs and put out the cheese Morna sent for the two of you. Then I'll be on my way. Good luck. It's going to be great."

He hoped with every breath that she was correct about that.

CHAPTER 29

I had debated over what to wear. It seemed important, somehow, that everything be just right for the occasion. In the end, I chose a blue summer-length dress that brought out the color of my eyes. It was comfy, casual, and in no way appropriate for the time period, but with everyone gone from the castle, I didn't think it really mattered.

Callum wore a kilt, his bare chest on glorious display. The only other time I'd seen him in such clothing was the night of the party, but he'd worn a shirt with it then. I wondered if he'd foregone the shirt on purpose, because he knew how gorgeous I'd think he looked without it. What he probably didn't realize is he looked gorgeous no matter what he did—or didn't—wear.

Everything was lovely—the castle looked amazing, the fire was warm, Callum's company was wonderful. Even Morna's cheese plate was an excellent addition. But, for the life of me, it seemed like Callum would never stop talking.

I loved talking to him. I really did. But we'd talked plenty over our last month together. I knew all about his family, his likes, his dislikes, his past adventures, and those he hoped to experience in the future. I knew his favorite foods and those he'd rather never eat again. I knew so many things about him. What I didn't know was why he'd not tried to move our relationship to the next level, romantically speaking.

I was fine with taking things slow, but I'd given him every signal that I was ready to move forward with this—more than ready. I couldn't understand his hesitation. Spending the night with Callum had been on my mind every second since he extended the invitation to me this afternoon. Why wasn't he making a move?

We kissed and cuddled by the fire, but he made no offer to move our "date" upstairs. We'd been curled up on a blanket in front of the fire in the sitting room for the better part of three hours. If he didn't do something soon, I feared I would fall asleep.

At this point, I couldn't even say for sure what he was talking about. My concentration had completely drifted away from the conversation. When I couldn't take any more of it, the question I'd been wondering all night bubbled out of me.

"Callum, why are we still moving so slowly? I mean . . . this thing between us. I've enjoyed the buildup, don't get me wrong. But I don't want it to last forever. Is something wrong?"

Confusion flickered across his face as my words pulled him out of his one-way conversation. "What?"

I scooted closer to him, placing one of my palms against his cheek as I leaned forward to kiss him. My lips shaped to his, and I traced the edge of his lower lip with my tongue until he pulled me tight against him. "I said...why are you still moving so slowly with our relationship? I wouldn't be here with you tonight if I still wanted to go slow." I pulled away, intent on having a real answer from him before the evening proceeded. He appeared rather shocked, and I couldn't tell if it was due to my question or the teasing kiss and quick pull away.

"Surely, ye doona think that I doona want ye?"

"No. I haven't been worried about that. I'm not worried about anything, really. I'm just curious. I know that you want us to be together, but you keep me at a distance in a way. I mean, I sense restraint in you, even when we're kissing. Why?"

"Come here, lass. Let me wrap my arms around ye."

I crawled over to him, nestling against him as he held me close. I loved the feeling of his arms surrounding me.

Callum heaved a heavy sigh. "Do ye mind if I tell ye a story?"

"Another one?"

He laughed and kissed me roughly on the cheek. "I'm sorry. I have been speaking too much, aye? Doona worry, this story ye will wish to hear."

"Okay." I laughed softly.

"The first time ye ever saw me was when I picked ye up at the airport, aye?"

"Yes."

"That is not the first time I saw ye."

I shifted in his arms, surprised. "No?"

He shook his head. "The first time I saw ye, I thought ye a ghost. Ye were in my bedchamber. I would only see short glimpses, and then ye would fade. Each time I was disappointed when ye left. Ghost or not, I fancied ye even then."

"Are you being serious?" While he seemed fond of the memory, the whole idea really freaked me out. "How is that possible? Firstly, I'm not a ghost. Secondly, how could you have seen me here months before I was actually here?"

He shrugged. "I doona know. The magic between this Cagair and the next links the two places. Sometimes images glimmer through, but they are always a reflection of what is truly happening on the other side. Yer image is the only one that differed. I saw ye before ye arrived, as if ye were destined to be here."

"I don't believe in destiny."

He shifted, turning me to face him more fully. "Aye, I know. Ye think, plan, and worry too much to believe that mayhap some people are meant to be together. I know ye, Sydney. I knew if I dinna tread carefully, if I dinna move slowly with ye, ye would run. Am I wrong?"

He wasn't wrong. I liked control. It was part of the reason I had distracted myself from anything resembling real life for so long. I could control work, but I was significantly less able to control my feelings. And it was the speed at which they developed for Callum that caused me to voice so many misgivings and questions at the beginning of our relationship. Oftentimes, I found that Callum seemed to have a better idea of what was going on inside me than I did.

"No. You're right. But I don't think if we took the next step, I would freak out and end things."

He grinned and shook his head before gathering my hands in his. "No, I doona think you would. There are other reasons I took my time, Sydney." He held my gaze. "Ye are far more special to me than any woman I've ever known before. I dinna wish to take ye to my bed until I made certain ye knew exactly how I felt about ye. And I had no intention of telling ye my feelings outright until I felt I could do so safely, without ye finding an excuse to put up a wall between us. I doona wish to lose ye."

"I love you." The words slipped out of my mouth quickly, before I took the time to consider whether or not they were wise, but I meant them completely. His reaction was not what I expected.

"Do ye say that only so I'll make love to ye, lass?"

"I want to make love with you, Callum, but I don't say things that I don't mean. I said it because I do love you, and I don't want you to think that I'm about to flee at any moment. I don't want you worrying. I'm finished holding anything back."

He stood. The change in his eyes was evident, the caring in

them replaced by desire. "Stand up, lass. Come with me, please. Ye know that I love ye. Now, let me show ye how much."

———

While Callum's room had clearly been lit by dozens of candles earlier in the evening, many of them had snuffed out during the course of his never-ending conversation with me downstairs. When we entered, only a few remained burning. They cast a pale light across the room that was as soft as Callum's touch.

He kept both hands on my arms as he walked me to the bed, pausing at the foot of it. "Do you know how long I've waited for you, Sydney?" he asked, turning me to face him.

I looked into his eyes. "Since that time you saw me here and thought I was a ghost?" I asked, my voice barely more than a whisper.

"Since then, yes, but also before."

"Before?"

He brushed a lock of hair off my cheek. "I feel as if I've waited all of my life for ye, as if I've always known you in my heart, and it was just a matter of time until we met."

I took a sharp breath as his fingertip trailed downward, skimming my cheek, my jaw, my neck, pausing at my collarbone to stroke it back and forth. His other hand came around to my back, and he slowly unzipped my dress. Stepping out of it, I placed a palm against his chest and moved my other hand up to his shoulder to the kilt strap that lay draped across his front. I was able to remove it from his shoulder, but when I went about trying to pull it off his waist, the effort turned into a bit of a comedy show. I tugged and pulled and even walked around behind him to see if I could figure out the trick. When I couldn't, I moved to stand in front of him again, crossing my arms in frustration.

"What's the matter with it? Do you have it glued on?" I asked.

"No, lass." Chuckling, he pressed a finger to my lips. "No more talking. We did enough of that earlier, doona ye think?."

Callum removed his kilt with ease. He didn't drop it carelessly to the floor as I had my dress. He gathered it up in front of him, folded it neatly and set it to the side, stepped back, leaving a small space between us.

He was beautiful—his body, his smile, the look in his eyes when they met mine.

In my experience, physically beautiful men usually had an ego the size of Cagair Castle. I was relieved that with Callum that wasn't the case. There was no shyness about him, but I sensed his vulnerability as my gaze swept over him. And when his gaze swept over me, his appreciation of what he saw was evident on his face.

With Callum, there would be no game playing, no guessing. He was like no man I'd ever met before. I knew instinctively that when we were intimate, it would be raw, honest, and real. What a relief. I'd had more than my fill of pretense and passive-aggressiveness from men. I was done with it.

Callum and I crossed the space separating us and stepped into each other's arms.

"I know ye think I move too slowly, but I'll not rush this, Sydney," he said, his hands moving over me. "I've waited too long to have it be over too soon."

Smiling, I said, "Take all the time you want."

His touch was tender, his kiss urgent, and soon I lost myself in the sensation.

We kissed, and touched and loved the night away, and it was sexy and sweet and delicious. Callum obviously wanted nothing more than to please me. And he did. But he also wanted to be pleased. With him, it was all about give and take.

I opened to him in a way I never had before. In my past, I had shared my body, but I had never shared my heart. I'd had sex, but had never made love until now. Until Callum.

He was worth the wait.

By the time we collapsed in each other's arms, so exhausted that we had no choice but to let sleep finally take us, I knew that I would never spend a night with any other man.

And that was just as I wished it.

CHAPTER 30

Callum hoped Sydney would sleep until midday. He knew she must be tired enough to do so. The simple fact that she'd not risen before the sun to go running was a sure sign of her exhaustion. He was tired as well, but with everyone still away enjoying a few days of rest, there was much that he needed to take care of on his own.

He slipped out of the bed carefully, making sure that his movements didn't wake her. When he stood, he could see Sydney's toes sticking from beneath the blankets. He moved around to the end of the bed to cover them before dressing and making his way outside.

His skin was still warm to the touch from holding Sydney as they slept in each other's arms. He expected the cool, outside breeze to soothe him. Instead, it seemed to hum with danger.

The moment he cleared the castle's main doorway, he ran toward the narrow pathway, watching for the rider whose approach he somehow sensed. It took only a moment for the rider to crest the small hill, and Callum immediately recognized the tartan he wore as that of the Conalls.

Callum continued to run toward the rider, and the man didn't slow the pace of his horse until they met in the middle. "What news have ye?"

The man didn't wait to dismount before saying, "The Conalls, sir. They were attacked on their way home as they neared the territory line. Yer uncle, Donal MacChristy, he…"

The man trailed off, and Callum's stomach turned over with dread. "What? He what, lad?"

"He is dead. The man tried to wound Blaire, and Donal jumped in to save his daughter. The attacker ran him straight through with a blade."

A sudden wave of loss crashed down on Callum. No one was more alive than Donal, especially with the excitement over his coming grandchild evident in his every jolly word. The loss was a great one. Callum's father, his brothers, Blaire, all of the Conalls would long be in grief before solace found them.

"Who? Who attacked them? Who would have reason to? Macaslan is dead."

"We doona know. There were five of them, and they all got away. 'Twas too sudden an attack for even great warriors such as Eoin and Arran to stop them. All we have to identify the men is this."

The rider dismounted and handed Callum a torn piece of tartan. He didn't recognize it, not enough to declare his knowledge to the rider, but a flicker of suspicion sparked within him, and every bone in his body grew cold.

Meeting Callum's gaze, the rider said, "They kept some of the cloth for themselves to help in the search, but they asked that I bring ye this in case ye might know it. Donal's burial is set for this morn. 'Tis all the news I have for ye. I must go back so I am there when the family is ready to continue their search for the attackers."

"Aye, o'course ye must. Tell Eoin that I will be in touch shortly. My men and I will aid in all efforts."

Callum waited only a moment before turning away from the

rider. He ran as quickly as his still-tight leg would allow. He called for Sydney as loudly as he could, hoping with every step she would hear and meet him so he wouldn't have to spend time retrieving her from his room.

He knew the moment he saw her running down the staircase that she must have awakened shortly after he did. Thankfully, she was already dressed.

"What's wrong? I could see the rider from the window."

"I doona have time to explain it to ye. There is something I must attend to this moment, and I canna leave ye here while I do it. I fear we are not safe after all."

She didn't question him further. Together they ran the short distance to the stairwell. When they made it through to the other side, he ordered her to go ahead of him.

"Go on, lass. I'll find ye as soon as I can and explain everything to ye. Right now, I must speak with Jane."

She kissed him, a brief touch of her lips that did much to calm his rattled nerves, then walked out of the stairwell away from him. He followed her into the castle, hoping with every step that Jane would still have what he sought.

He waited until Sydney turned down into the kitchen, and then he hurried upstairs toward his brother and sister-in-law's bedchamber. The light was still off inside. He hoped his entry wouldn't disturb Nora if she still slept.

Callum knocked once and pushed the door open as calmly as he could manage, calling out to make his presence known.

"Jane, are ye in here? I doona wish to wake the babe."

"Come in." Jane ushered him in with a whisper. As he stepped inside, he could see that all wasn't truly dark inside the room. Jane sat near the window, a small lamp lighting the seat where she held the bottle-suckling Nora in her arms.

"Jane, I'm sorry to disturb ye, but I must ask something of ye straight away. The blanket that was wrapped around Nora the day of the fire...did ye keep it? Tell me ye did."

Callum watched as concern spread across Jane's face. She stood, still cradling the child.

"I did. It's in the keepsake box I started for her. If you'll take her, I'll grab it. What is going on?"

"I just received word that the Conalls were attacked as they neared home. Donal was killed, and no one recognizes the tartan on those that attacked them."

Jane's eyes widened in recognition. "No...you don't think? Surely not."

Callum moved to balance Nora in one arm so that he could retrieve the torn cloth from the edge of his kilt with his free hand. "I doona know, Jane. 'Tis why I need ye to retrieve the blanket for me. Does it match this?"

Jane said nothing until she stood up from the small chest on the opposite side of the room. When she faced him, her face was red with rage.

The blanket and piece of kilt were a perfect match.

"That . . ." she hissed. "I'd like to send Laird Allen straight to hell."

Callum took the blanket from Jane's trembling hand, his mind reeling from the betrayal. "Oh, to hell he will go, lass. But 'twill be my hands that send him there."

CHAPTER 31

My heart ached for everyone who knew Donal MacChristy, but none more so than Blaire. All I could think of was the last kitchen conversation I had with her. She told me all about her years-long struggle to get pregnant and how Donal was counting the days until he could hold his grandson—Donal was certain she carried a boy—in his arms.

Perfect in his timing, he'd appeared in the kitchen doorway, and the first thing he did was spin her chair around so that he could bend and speak to the child.

"'Tis me again, laddie, yer Grandpapa. I canna wait to count all of yer fingers and toes." He'd stood and addressed me, as if feeling the need to explain. *"I mean to make certain the child knows my voice the moment he arrives in this world. Ach, how my wife would have loved a grandchild."*

I choked up thinking back on the moment, and tears fell freely as I hurried to turn away from Callum. He was in the midst of his own grief over Donal's death. I didn't want him worrying over my own sadness. My heart didn't hurt for any feeling of self-loss; I hurt for Blaire and how devastating the loss would be to her. And I hurt for Donal and the dream he lost that day by protecting the unborn baby he already loved so much.

"Ye needn't hide yer tears from me, lass," said Callum. "Many will be shed in these halls over the next days."

"My heart is broken for her. For her to have wished and prayed and hoped for a baby for so long—the baby's birth should only be filled with joy for her. Now sorrow will be just as present on that day."

I turned toward him, moving to wrap myself up in his open arms. He was shaken from the day's events, but he remained strong for everyone. I got the impression it was his normal way of handling things.

"Aye it will, and there was no reason that it should be so. No matter how many times I turn it all over in my mind, I canna make sense of it. What reason would Laird Allen have?"

I couldn't begin to imagine. Only the day before, everyone in the castle had been singing the man's praises. None of it fit together well in my mind. Like Callum, I couldn't arrange all of the separate pieces into any semblance of reason. It worried me. For him to have his men conduct such an outright attack surely meant he was only getting started.

"I don't know, Callum. What will you do?"

When he spoke, his voice was weary. "'Tis no longer my decision alone on how we progress. More information is needed before any of us decides how to move forward. I could almost understand if his ill will was toward me, for no matter the truth of it, I feel responsible for the death of his brother. It wouldna be surprising for him to blame me for that, but for him to attack the Conalls only muddles everything."

I wished there was more I could do to help him. "Who will decide what to do then?" I asked. "How will you gather more information?"

He released me and moved to sit by the fire. "With the Conalls already home, we canna verra well consult with them at this time. But there are still plenty of us here to represent our allied clans. Everyone here knew Donal. This day will be for grieving his loss. Tomorrow morning all of us will meet and make plans."

I could see by the way he sat in his chair—with his back hunched so that he could rest his chin on one clenched fist—that while he would wait for everyone's advisement and agreement, he'd already made plans of his own.

"What will you suggest come morning?"

"In truth, I doona know. Wisdom seems to have left me this eve. I am simply hoping that one among us will find the words that I have not. I only know what I'm about to tell ye. I hope ye will understand. Laird Allen's actions make it clear to me that Cagair Castle is no safer now than it was before the fire. I'll not leave my home unattended again. I'll not risk the same thing happening twice. While I've instructed all workers to stay away, I'll be sleeping in my home this night."

It was the last thing I wanted him to do. While part of me wanted to beg him to stay here in this time where he was surely safe, it would go against everything I had made clear to him from the very first. We were each to have our own lives. I couldn't tell him what to do if I expected him to give me the same courtesy.

I nodded. "Just tell me you're not staying all alone."

"Orick will join me since he's yet to have any children. Tom has insisted that he stay as well. I've no reason to believe anything will happen, but if it should, I'll not be away this time."

"I understand." And I did, no matter how much it pained me. "Callum, can I ask you something?"

He looked up and gave me a gentle smile. "O'course ye can. Never hesitate to ask me anything."

"I know that for so long you didn't want me going back with you—not until Macaslan was dead. And I know you told me last night that part of your hesitation was born from your fear that anything too quick would scare me away, but I think there was more to it than that. I think that you hesitated because you were worried that you wouldn't be able to protect me. Like you said just a minute ago, you feel responsible for the fire. I think you knew that if something ever happened to me, you would blame yourself. Am I right?" I could tell from the knowing glint in his eyes that I was.

"Aye, lass. I couldna bear it. The guilt and sorrow would eat me alive."

I nodded and moved out of my seat to crouch down beside him, reaching for both of his hands. "I know, but it wouldn't be your fault. I want you to know that. Even though you love me, you are not responsible for me. So please, Callum, don't use your fear over everything that happened to push me away. Tell me you won't."

He lowered his head to mine, and the need in his kiss was one of comfort rather than lust. "Lass, might we make each other a promise, ye and I? I willna distance myself from ye, though for now, I'll not be around ye as much as I'd like. I promise ye that when all of this is over, I'll want ye as much as I do now. Now, will ye make me a promise as well?"

"What is it?"

"I know ye told me that ye doona want me telling ye what to do, but in this instance please doona take offense to it. 'Twill ease much of my suffering if ye agree to it. I beg of ye, Sydney, swear to me that ye will not enter my time again until we know the truth of what is happening with Laird Allen, and he has been brought to justice."

All he wanted was for me to be safe, but even in times of peace, safety was never a guarantee—that was just the way with life. "Callum, what if that takes years?"

"It willna take years, lass. I fully intend for all of this to be over within a fortnight. Just promise me, for now, that ye will stay safely here so I can see to the safety of others without worrying about ye as well."

There would be much to attend to here. Regardless of the plans that were made in the morning, I knew that lots of little ones would remain here to ensure their safety. My hands, and the hands of anyone else around, would be full. If it truly was just for now, it seemed a simple enough promise to keep.

"Okay. I promise. I will stay right here until you tell me it is safe to return to you again."

CHAPTER 32

"Isent a group of men out this morning to search for answers. I expect the Conalls are already doing the same, and we will hear something from them soon."

I sat at the back of the sitting room with Cooper on one side of me and Jerry on the other. Everyone seemed to be in various stages of worry and grief. The atmosphere in the room hung heavy over all of us as Callum led the discussion.

He spoke for a long while, filling everyone in on the current situation. All were quiet while he spoke. Only when he finished did Laird McMillan—Baodan—rise to address Callum.

"I think it best that I, my brother, and Jeffrey leave for home to make certain no similar attacks are attempted in our own territory, though I doona think it wise for us to do so on horseback." Baodan turned and directed his gaze toward Morna. "Can we still travel back at the McMillan Castle of this time? If so, would ye be willing to take us there and see us through today?"

Morna nodded. I could see from her unsurprised expression that perhaps the thought had already occurred to her. "Aye. I'll leave with ye lads today. Why doona yer wives and children come to stay with me and Jerry for a time? 'Twill be easier for ye to send word to me when things are safe if I am home—I've more powers at my disposal there. When I know that 'tis safe for them, and ye've let me know ye are ready for them to return, I can send them back. Jerry can go with the others tomorrow so they have time to prepare."

Baodan glanced first at Mitsy then over at Eoghanan and Grace, followed by Jeffrey and Kathleen. When they all gave their agreement, Baodan turned back toward Callum. "Does the arrangement suit ye?"

Callum gave his approval and continued to hash things out with everyone else in the room.

At Morna's mention of their return home, I noticed Jerry stiffen in his seat next to me. Once the room began to hum with the noise of many separate conversations, I turned to ask him about it. "Is everything all right?"

"No, but I canna discuss it with ye here. Once Morna leaves with the others, come and find me."

Jerry stood and silently slipped from the room.

"*P*lease promise me that ye will be careful, Callum. Ye doona know how much I care for ye. When all is over, ye will come and see me, aye?"

Callum held Morna close to him, squeezing the old witch tightly enough that her toes lifted off the ground.

"Aye, Morna, I do think I know, for I care for ye just as much. I shall see ye soon. Ye must be glad to be going home, aye? Ye threw a mighty fit when we wouldna let ye do so after Jerry's attack."

Morna blushed slightly, and Callum thought it the first time he'd ever seen her do so. "I am ready to sleep in my own bed, but I am not glad for the circumstances that have me leaving here today."

He released his grip on her, gave her a quick kiss on the cheek, and reached for the car door to open it for her.

Rather than climb inside, Morna grabbed his arm and pulled him away from the car. "Hold on just a moment. There's something I wish to tell ye before I go."

He moved to lace her arm with his own, escorting her away from the crowd as she clearly wished him to. "What is it, Morna?"

"I want to thank ye, not only for remaining kind to me in the midst of some verra bad behavior on my part, but also for being one of the few lads I've ever known to not do exactly what I told ye to."

Callum frowned, trying to think on what the witch could mean. His mind was too filled with Laird Allen, with the Conalls, and with trying to figure out all he didn't understand, to remember what Morna referred to. "What do ye mean by that? Are ye pointing to a specific instance?"

"Aye, verra specific, indeed. Do ye not remember when I asked ye to search for Grier? Ye told me ye wouldna do so unless ye had cause. I thought Jerry's heart attack was plenty cause enough, and still ye denied my request."

In truth, he'd never stopped his search for the witch. Morna didn't know that the dance had been a failed trap to catch her. She didn't know that he'd had a man searching day and night for Grier since the morning after Jerry's heart attack. Callum knew it was best she didn't know because the witch had not been found.

"And ye are happy about that?" he asked her. "It surprises me to hear ye say so. I thought ye were still rather sour about all of it."

The old witch shrugged and reached with her free hand to pat his arm. "I would've thought so, too, but I find I'm quite pleased that ye dinna do as I asked. It seems that Grier has given up on whatever it was she wanted with Jerry and me. I couldna be more glad for it. 'Tis only here that she could reach us. My departure today means it has come to an end."

At least one set of problems had reached a resolution. He was no longer concerned with his search for Grier either. There were much more pressing matters at hand. "I am glad for it, as well. Though I still protest that she is not as bad as ye remember her to be. She helped me the day of the fire. Whether ye wish to believe it or not, I believe she saved Jerry's life on the day of his attack."

Callum knew Jerry had tried to make Morna see sense on the matter, but she refused to believe anything but the worst of Grier despite his pleas. Callum expected the same reaction.

"'Tis true that I'm not sure I know anymore," Morna said, surprising Callum. Squeezing his arm a little more tightly, she added, "As much as I've held on to the hatred I have of her, there was a time that I loved her verra much. I admit that I thought Jerry's defense of her was born out of his trusting nature. Perhaps this time it was only because he was right. Either way, I am at peace not knowing."

Believing her to be finished, Callum slowly led them back toward the car. "Peace is all I wish for all of us, Morna. I pray that it finds us soon."

She turned to hug him one last time in farewell. "Oh, I do too, lad. I do too."

CHAPTER 33

Fatigue descended quickly upon everyone at the castle after Morna left with the McMillan men. Even Cooper, known for his insomnia, took a nap. I attempted to do so as well, only remembering as my eyes were nearly closed that Jerry had asked me to find him.

I could sleep later. As concerned as Jerry had appeared earlier, I didn't wish to keep him waiting.

I stood and did a few lengthy stretches for energy and crossed the hall to his room.

He didn't answer at my first knock, and I wondered if perhaps he was napping as well. When no response came the second time, I opened the door to look inside. The room was empty.

My first thought was that perhaps he was off looking for me. While I thought it odd that he wouldn't check my room first, I made my way down to the kitchen to check for him there. All I found was a pile of dirty dishes awaiting my attention.

They would just have to wait longer, for now my curiosity—as well as my concern—was at an all-time high. Where could he have wandered off to?

I looked everywhere that I could without disturbing sleeping babies or moms, and eventually decided to search for him outside. It didn't take me long to approach the stairwell and, much to my surprise, I found him sitting on a step halfway down.

"Jerry," I called out to him as I approached.

He turned around casually, as if nothing were odd about his location. "Ach, Sydney. There ye are, lass. I thought perhaps ye forgot my request that ye seek me out."

"I'll admit I forgot for a moment, but I thought you meant to meet you in your room. What are you doing out here?"

He stood and took one more step down the staircase. "I am simply doing precisely what I told ye I would do. Today is the day I was meant to trick Morna into traveling through. Grier waits for us on the other side. While Morna canna go, I must."

My heart jumped into my throat. "No way. Get back up here, Jerry, or I will drag you up these stairs myself. You can't be serious? Surely you know with everything that happened that you have to forget about this right now. You can come back another time and try to heal the bad blood between Morna and Grier."

He shook his head and took another step downward. "No, Sydney. I broke a promise to Grier once before. I'll not do it again. I only asked ye to find me so ye could stand from this side and wait for me. If anything goes wrong, ye can call for help. I will do this regardless of yer thoughts on the matter. Will ye wait and watch for me or not? I willna be long."

I took two steps down into the stairwell myself, then stopped when I saw that he meant to run through if I approached him. "Jerry, wait. Just think about this for a minute. No one is through there. Callum and Orick won't be back through until tonight. At least wait until then."

He held up a hand to stop me from taking another step forward. "No. I canna wait, for I willna make Grier wait. I'll ask ye one last time. Then I go either way. Will ye wait and watch for me?"

I groaned and gripped my forehead to push away the sudden

pounding pain. I didn't think I could take any more stress today. Clearly, there was no fighting him on this. If he was going, I could at least be here to escort him out when he returned.

"Fine. You have ten minutes. If you're not back by then, I'm getting Callum."

He picked up one foot as he twisted to look over his shoulder at me, but his words were cut short as he tripped over the next step and began to tumble downward. Everything slowed down as he fell, but I couldn't reach him in time.

Jerry picked up speed as he rolled. Even as he reached the bottom, he continued to skid until he hit the wall and disappeared.

I screamed and closed my eyes in painful surrender of what I knew I must do.

Most likely, Jerry was injured. What if Grier hadn't kept her word to him? What if no one was on the other side? I couldn't leave him there bleeding and alone. Callum would just have to forgive me.

I took the steps down two at a time and vanished into dust.

CHAPTER 34

1650

"Jerry, are you okay? You are a stupid, stupid fool. I told you this was a terrible idea. Give me your hand so I can help you out of here and back to our own time. There's no one around to stitch you up here."

I couldn't see him, and his lack of response worried me greatly. The stairwell was completely dark, and I hadn't the slightest idea why. I supposed it probably had some sort of door, but the entire time I'd known about it, I'd never seen it closed.

I called out to him once more, only to have a hand latch over my mouth to silence me.

"Can ye not tell that we closed the door for a reason?" a woman's voice said. "Jerry is bleeding, but there is not time for me to do anything for it now. Ye surely have drawn their attention to us. Laird Allen's men are besieging the castle as I speak."

She released her grip on me. While I knew it wiser for me to stay quiet, I couldn't stand there and say nothing. Terror and confusion gripped at me, and it took every bit of strength I had not to panic. "Jerry, get up. We have to go back through."

The stranger's arm—which I assumed belonged to Grier—shot out and yanked me backward toward the steps. "There's no time. They're already here. I see them."

That instant, the door to the stairwell swung open and light streamed in. I struggled to adjust to the quick onset of light as bellowing voices hollered down at us. "Down here, sir. There are people hiding."

The man stepped away, and I hurried to pull Jerry up so we could run back through. Grier blocked our way. "Can ye not see? They've seen us. If we go through the portal now, they will follow us through. Is that what ye want?"

In my panic, that thought hadn't occurred to me. All I could think of was how desperately we needed to get away. I knew Callum would never recover if anything happened to either Jerry or me. The guilt and grief would destroy him.

"Can you close it? Let us run through and then close it before Laird Allen's men have a chance to go through. We can't let them take us."

She shook her head. "I canna close it from that side."

The calm on her face did nothing to soothe me. She looked as if all of it were pointless.

"They will take us," Grier added. "We must allow them to do so lest we wish to end up murdered this day."

For the second time in a matter of moments, everything around me seemed to slow down, making every thought calm and clear. "Can't you use magic to stop them?"

"I'm powerful, but no. I canna take down two dozen men. Listen to me. When they take us, they canna know I'm a witch. It willna end well for me, and I'll be no help to either of ye if they do."

I knew she was right. If Laird Allen learned of Grier's powers, he would either force her to use them for his will, or kill her outright.

I thought of Jerry's fall down the stairs. While I couldn't see him, I knew his wounds must be significant, for he said nothing as Grier and I spoke. Someone would have to carry him up the stairs. By doing so, they risked traveling forward. I knew by watching others, only the smallest part of you had to touch the back wall for it to pull you forward.

"Grier, can you close the portal from this side? We need to be certain they can't get through."

She didn't answer right away. When she did, her voice was small and surprisingly unsure. "I doona know."

"Do you have time to try?"

"I doona. They're coming now. If I do so, they'll see me."

They might see her, but she must try. Otherwise, we risked the lives of so many others. "I'll run up and distract them. Try and close it."

I ran up the stairs and busted through the door while screaming like a banshee. It took a moment for my eyes to adjust to the sudden sunlight. When they did, I saw six giant men hurtling toward me.

As they pulled at my arms and began to drag me away, I swung and kicked my legs in every possible direction. I would be bruised and bloodied and very possibly dead, but at least Grier now had a few more moments to close the portal, hopefully keeping everyone at Cagair in the twenty-first century safe from harm.

CHAPTER 35

Present Day

It wasn't like Sydney to rest so late in the afternoon, but everyone was more tired than usual today, and Callum knew there was good reason for it. "Sydney, I doona wish to disturb ye, but Orick and I are headed through, and Adwen, as well, this time," he said to her through the darkness. "I doona think we will be returning—not until we've answers, and all of this with Laird Allen has reached its end. I wanted to tell ye goodbye."

He walked quietly across the floor, then flipped on the small lamp next to her bedside so he could wake her gently.

The covers were crinkled, the indentation of her body still present, but she was no longer in the bed. Callum glanced at the clock in the corner of the room. She would be deep in dinner preparations now. He stood and made his way there to bid her farewell.

When he reached the kitchen, the only one inside was Anne.

"Hey, are you guys about to head back?" she asked.

"Aye. Do ye know where Sydney is, Anne? I wish to tell her goodbye before we leave. It may be some weeks before we return. She was not in her bedchamber."

Anne pursed her lips in a way that sent a shudder down his spine. "I...I was just about to ask you about her. I wondered if maybe she was sick or something because she is usually already in the kitchen by now. I was about to attempt to start on something myself. You haven't seen her?"

"No. Not in some time."

Callum turned to the sound of footsteps behind him. "Cooper, what brings ye into the kitchen. Are ye hungry? I bet Anne could find ye something."

"No, I'm not hungry. I came here looking for you, Callum. I've got a really funny feeling about something. Sydney comes and gets me every day to help Jerry workout, and this was supposed to be our very last time before he returned home, but she never came and got me. I waited an hour. Now I can't find Jerry, either. I've looked everywhere for both of them, and I can't find them anywhere."

The fear he struggled to keep at bay every moment rose up inside him. "Are ye certain, lad? Is there any place in the castle that ye have not looked?"

Cooper shook his head, his eyes wide and serious. "No. I looked everywhere in the castle. The only place I haven't been is outside, but Jerry never goes out there, so I thought it would be a waste."

Callum allowed himself a deep, calming breath at Cooper's words. Surely if he hadn't checked outside, then outside was where he would find them.

"Cooper, ye stay here and help Anne begin dinner. I'll go and look for them outside. I'll be certain to let them know ye are not pleased when I find them."

"Yeah, you tell them that because I am not pleased at all."

Callum hurried from the kitchen, eager to find them so his worry would subside.

Rather than opening the main door to find Jerry and Sydney, Adwen stood in the doorway. "Callum, ye best come. Something has happened."

He could feel the blood drain from his face at Adwen's words. How much more could happen? How much more could they possibly bear? "What? Tell me now."

Adwen turned and waved for him to follow. "The portal. It...it doesna seem to be working."

Callum had traveled through only a matter of hours ago. He was only in the twenty-first century now to see Morna and the McMillan men off. "Ye're wrong. I used it not long ago. How could it stop working?"

"I doona know, but I swear to ye, it's shut. I dinna feel comfortable with all of us being on this side, even if it was for such a brief time. I thought I would go ahead and watch for messengers until ye and Orick arrived. Callum, 'tis nothing at the bottom but a stone wall."

His heart pounded in his chest as he hurried down the all-too-familiar steps. Adwen must be mistaken. If he wasn't, something was very wrong.

He stopped at the bottom step and cautiously reached out his fingers. The wall ahead of him was solid.

Callum turned and ran up the stairs as quickly as he had descended them. "Go and tell everyone to search for Sydney and Jerry. Now."

Adwen turned from him, and Callum ran for the castle behind him, shouting to Orick, who was just exiting his cottage.

The entire castle spent the better part of an hour searching. When every last corner had been covered, Callum collapsed on the castle's front steps, allowing his anger to take him as Adwen, Orick, and Anne watched on.

"Blast her. She told me she wouldna do it. She swore to me,

and she did it anyway. I'll not have her near me again. I'll not share my heart with a liar and a fool. I doona understand what she's done or why, but she and Jerry traveled through the portal, and now 'tis closed for the rest of us."

He continued to lament, screaming and cursing, using his anger as a way to keep his worry from consuming him.

Anne stepped in front of him and reached up to grab both sides of his face tightly between her hands. "All right. I let you have a good five minutes of that, but it is time to grow up. You're right. You don't know why she and Jerry went back, but Sydney is no idiot. If she did so, she had reason to, and you know it. I know you're frightened, but this temper tantrum will do you no good. You don't have time for it. Laird Allen could be headed for Cagair now. What if he finds them there?"

He started to speak but was rewarded with a quick smack from Anne's palm.

"No. Be quiet and listen to me. You boys must get back as quickly as you can. You can't do that here, so take my keys and drive as quickly as you can for McMillan Castle. As slow as Morna drives, you may be able to reach it before she leaves."

"Yer right."

"Of course, I'm right." Anne paused, stood, and reached for the keys in her pocket before placing them in his hand and giving him a good shove toward the car. "I'm serious. Get out of here now. And if all three of you—in fact—if everyone else that is back there that we know and love doesn't get out of this thing alive and well, I will never forgive any of you. Now get."

Callum grunted as she kicked him in his bum for good measure. Without another word, the three men loaded into the car and raced away from Cagair Castle.

There was no time to waste.

CHAPTER 36

On The Road To Macaslan Castle—1650

"Oy, there ye are. I'm glad to see ye awake. I feared perhaps ye truly injured yerself. I've never seen anyone throw themselves about in such a manner."

My eyes flickered open slowly, and I struggled to keep them from closing once more from the pain in my head. My hands were bound between my legs, and I rode in front of a man I didn't know on a horse so large in size my thighs ached dreadfully from spreading them so wide.

"Injured myself? Is that how you see it? I was dragged and bound and knocked unconscious. I'm not sure how I could manage that myself."

"Ach, I like that ye've still got bite after the fight ye put up. I doona care how ye remember it, lass. Neither I, nor any of my men, harmed ye in any way. We simply tried to stop yer screaming. Ye thrashed about such that ye managed to hit yer head on the blunt side of one of my men's swords. Ye'll have a mighty bruise from it, but otherwise ye seem to be fine."

I twisted slightly, and I could see that the man I rode with led the group of men behind us. I couldn't see Jerry or Grier anywhere, and I said a silent prayer for their safety as I turned to look up at my captor.

He had dark eyes and hair, a full beard, and a sharp slant to his nose that only added to his intimidating appearance.

"So, what...you didn't injure me now just so you could do so later?" I laced my voice with as much venom and sarcasm as I could manage. My head pounded, and it irritated me to no end that he found it amusing.

"Ye've a verra poor impression of me, lass. I must say that I canna see a reason for it. We arrived just in time to rescue ye from far worse hands."

Rescue me? I sat quietly for a moment, toying with the idea in my mind. Was it possible that I was wrong about this man's identity?

"I'm sorry. I think maybe I'm confused. You are Laird Allen, aren't you?"

He laughed against my ear, and I leaned forward dramatically to keep his breath from touching my neck.

"Aye, one and the same, though I am still not accustomed to being referred to as laird. Please, call me Raudrich. If ye promise me ye willna try to throw yerself off this horse, I'll untie yer hands."

"I can't promise you anything. If you wish to keep that nose so perfectly sculpted, you better keep me tied up."

"Oh, I like ye, lass. Too bad Callum's already claimed ye as his own."

"How would you know that? And don't tell me you rescued us from anything. We know what you did. We know what you did to the Conalls."

He stiffened behind me. For a moment, I feared I was too free with my words. I was, after all, helpless in this situation. If he wished to harm me, there was nothing I could do about it. Instead, when he spoke, his voice was soft and questioning.

"The Conalls? Has something happened to them? The men with me now were stationed around the Conall territory to help guard it for weeks. I only met with them again this afternoon as we approached Cagair."

My heart surged with anger and fear at the realization that the very men behind me were the ones who had killed Donal. "You can't be serious!"

He bent and lowered his voice as he whispered his answer. "Aye, lass, I couldna be more serious. Might I suggest that ye tell me exactly what happened? If ye are wise, ye will do so quietly. 'Tis clear that events have occurred without my knowing. I suddenly feel the need to be on guard."

"Where are the others I was with when you kidnapped me?" I ignored his question for now. If he didn't know—and I didn't possibly see how he couldn't—I would have to be sure Grier and Jerry were safe before I told him anything more.

"I let them go. The man's head was bleeding, and not one of my men can sew a stitch for anything. The woman claimed she would help him, so we saw them to her home before we left with ye. I've no need of them as long as they're safe. I doona believe they are the ones that Drustan Macaslan desires to harm."

"What does that mean?" I hadn't the slightest idea who Drustan Macaslan was, although I assumed him to be a relative of the late Laird Macaslan.

"Tit for tat, lass. I told ye precisely where yer friends were. Now ye must tell me what happened with the Conalls, and do so quickly and quietly. Then I will answer yer question, and ye will answer another of mine, and so we shall go until either we reach our destination or I decide how we must proceed."

I huffed but could see no other way around it. With each new word that came out of Raudrich's mouth, I grew more confused.

He had been a hero who, within a day, turned into our greatest enemy. I should hate him, but I found I liked him more by the minute.

"Your men attacked the Conalls as they approached their home. Donal MacChristy was killed and several other men wounded."

He grabbed onto my bound hands and squeezed them urgently.

"Doona say another word. I beg ye to follow my lead."

I nodded in understanding, trusting him despite every reason I had not to. He leaned back away from me and called out to the men lagging a short distance behind us.

"The lass says she needs to relieve herself. All of ye dismount and rest a few moments. I'll walk her further out so she has a moment of privacy."

There were words of understanding and agreement all around. As Laird Allen pulled his horse to a stop, he slid off the back and then turned to assist me. The moment my feet touched the ground, he hurried to undo my bindings, grabbing one of my hands as he finished to lead me away.

He said nothing but moved quickly through the thick woods and brush. He didn't stop until we were so far away that I knew his men couldn't hear our conversation.

"What is yer name, lass?"

"Sydney." I rubbed my sore wrists as he released my hand.

"I doona know what ye were told, but I dinna order the attack on the Conalls. I've done naught but work to keep peace throughout the Highlands my entire life. These men betrayed me. Whether it be for money or hatred, I doona know, but if they did as ye say, only to return to my side..."

His words drifted to an end as he paused and paced around me. As if the short movement helped him gather his thoughts, he turned in front of me and spoke once more.

"If they attacked the Conalls, we are not safe in their

presence. I know these woods well. I can manage to get away from them, but ye must stand where ye are and doona resist me pulling ye up when I reach for ye."

He placed his fingers on the edges of his mouth and let loose a loud whistle that left my ears ringing. He ran away from me, and I could hear the hooves coming toward us as he hurried to meet his charging horse. Raudrich mounted the beast with ease as the horse passed by. Before I realized what he'd meant, he scooped me up and onto the back of his horse so that I sat in front of him.

"Where are we going?"

"To Macaslan Castle, lass. 'Tis where the rest of my men await us. Let us both pray that there are more betrayers behind us than those we may find ahead."

CHAPTER 37

McMillan Castle—Present Day

Callum watched with surprise as Morna fondled the rocks in her hands. Adwen had already passed through, followed shortly by Orick. Only he and Morna remained on the shores of McMillan Castle's great pond. He couldn't believe she was truly planning to travel back with them.

"Ye'll wait for me, aye? When ye get through? Doona go running off toward the castle. Stay in the water and help me to the shore when I make my splash. I havena swam in over fifty years. I'm not certain I know how anymore."

Callum crossed his arms and glared at the ever-changeable witch.

"Do ye speak in jest, Morna? For I've not the time nor am I in the humor for it. How many times have I heard ye say ye would never be going back again? Not for anything, ye have always said."

She practiced skipping stones while she spoke.

"I'm not teasing ye in any way, Callum. I know what I said, but

I never thought for a moment that my husband, a man who has been terrified of my time period since we were young, would venture off through that portal with yer girlfriend. I'll not leave him there to be taken or injured by Laird Allen. I've been back before—ye can ask Cooper about that if ye are ever so inclined. While I doona like it, I canna see another way around it. Now, skip yer damn stone. I'll follow ye shortly."

Callum was eager to be on his way. The moment his water-soaked feet touched the ground of his own time, he would be ready to leave in search of Sydney. He didn't know whether he wanted to strangle or marry her when they next met, but he intended to find out very soon.

Macaslan Castle—Three Days Later—1650

"No. Get your hands off of me," I told Raudrich. "If you think I'm going to go in that castle with you after you covered me with hay and told me to stay put in this stable with your horse—who clearly has a serious case of IBS, by the way—then you are out of your mind. Why did you do that?"

I sat with my head buried in my shirt, trying to filter air that smelled exactly like a horse's bum. It was an unsuccessful effort.

"If ye will stand up and follow me while no one is watching, I will explain everything to ye in just a moment. I've food waiting for ye in my room."

The mention of food was the only thing that lured me from my corner. Raudrich made certain to tell the stable master that no one was to go near his horse except him, so I was able to hang out in the stall unseen, but I wasn't sure that my nose or my allergies would ever recover.

He covered me with a black cloak as we entered a secluded side door to the castle and rushed me quickly to his room so that we would be unseen. After closing the door behind us, he pointed at the gown on the bed.

"Put that on, Sydney." He went to a corner of the room and stood with his back turned away from me to give me privacy.

Until he mentioned it, I'd forgotten all about my modern clothes. I couldn't imagine what he or his men, regardless of whether they were traitors, had thought of my getup. They wouldn't know anything about where I came from.

Feeling very inappropriate, I did as he suggested and dressed quickly while keeping a close watch on his back. He remained a gentleman, never turning for even the shortest of glances while I changed.

After deserting the men Raudrich believed betrayed him, we had pushed hard night and day to reach Macaslan Castle, only stopping for necessary potty breaks. I couldn't believe the man's stamina. Nor could I believe it of his horse—both of them seemed completely otherworldly to me. He'd literally not slept a moment. He encouraged me to rest often during our travels, allowing me to lean against him as we rode. He had explained little during our journey. Now that we were finally here, I expected him to give me a full breakdown of everything.

"All right. I'm dressed. Now, why did you feel the need for me to spend the better part of the evening with your horse?"

"What did Callum tell ye about Drustan Macaslan, lass?"

"Is he the laird's son?"

"Aye."

I shrugged and told him the little I knew. "Only that he was just as evil-hearted as his father but far less capable of doing anything. I know that Laird Macaslan tried to marry Gillian—you probably don't know her—to Drustan, but Callum told him she was marrying him. The debacle over all of that is what started everything."

It was so strange to me that he seemed completely unsurprised by everything I said. Before he could ask another question, I jumped in again.

"You knew all that, didn't you. How? Callum said that your clan lives so far north nobody ever sees you. You also knew that I was with Callum. How did you know that?"

He gestured to the plate of food he'd prepared for me, and I moved to devour it.

"Callum is right that most of my clan lives in our territory far north, but I havena lived there in nearly fifteen years. It is not important that ye know where I *have* been, but I havena been home. Still, I make certain to keep abreast of all that goes on among the territories in the Highlands, though oftentimes it takes news longer to reach me. 'Tis why so much time passed from the fire to when I arrived at Cagair to pick up the remains of my brother and his wife. I not only had to learn of the news myself, I also had to gather his men and take my place as laird after their deaths."

He moved to sit by me, then continued, "All ye said about Drustan is true with only one exception. I believe Callum underestimates the lad greatly. I see now he is capable of doing far more harm than his father ever could. The two of us must stop him."

He reached over to tear a chunk of bread off of the loaf on my plate, popping it casually into his mouth and leaning back as if waiting for a reaction from me.

I rolled my hand and spoke with my mouth full. "Continue."

"Verra well. Every word I said to Callum the day I met him was the truth. My men and I searched high and low for Macaslan, but we never found him. He was not in Spain. When we knew that for certain, I came to this castle myself only to find a verra distraught Drustan who claimed his father had been missing for days. He'd not told anyone out of fear others would try to take his land if they knew his father was gone. I was much the fool to believe him."

I took a sip of wine to wash down my food. "So what was the truth?"

"Macaslan's last journey from this castle was the day he set fire to Cagair and murdered my brother and sister-in-law. When he returned here, Drustan had stormed his father's coffers and paid a large group of men enough money to turn against his father. They locked him away and kept him here until his death would be useful. Without knowing my role in any of this, I gave Drustan the perfect excuse to kill his father."

"How do you know? Surely he didn't tell you all of that?"

"No, he dinna. I spoke with my most trusted men, and they told me all that they know. I believe them. 'Twas only a small group that turned against me. The rest stayed here to await my orders."

"Why were any of your men here in the first place?"

Raudrich looked down at his feet, and I knew he most likely asked himself the same question. "I believed Drustan's fear was genuine, so I left many of my men to aid his own men in defense of this castle should word spread that Laird Macaslan was missing rather than in hiding. By doing so, the effect was two-fold. Drustan was not only able to pay some of my men enough money that they delivered his father's insignia to Callum, but also enough that they were willing to turn against me completely and attack the Conalls to start a war among our clans."

I slowed my eating as I listened. I wanted to carefully process every word he said. "So he started off simply wanting his father's territory for his own, but greed got the best of him? He hoped by securing his position here and then turning Callum's clan and the Conalls against you that he could take over yours as well?"

Raudrich nodded and stood to refill my glass. "Aye, I believe so. When I returned from Spain, I was riding for Cagair to inform Callum that my search had failed. I dinna know Macaslan was dead until ye told me. My men dinna tell me even as they met with me on the path and rode with me toward Callum's castle. When I arrived at Cagair to find it empty, I feared that Macaslan had either already returned or all had fled knowing he was on his way. That is why I thought I was rescuing ye. I thought ye and the others were hiding because ye knew Macaslan was coming."

"I see."

He stopped, stood, and started pacing as he had done in the forest. "Why were ye hiding, lass? And why was the castle empty if ye all knew Macaslan was dead?"

I couldn't very well tell him the truth, so I sat pensively for a long moment as I tried to figure out the answer that made the most sense, knowing what I did now. With the portal closed, I knew Callum would have to travel back at McMillan Castle, just as the other men intended to do.

"Cagair territory is small, and Callum didn't think he would have enough men. He knew that the Conalls were too deep in grief and too far away to be of much help so he went to gather the McMillans. He expected that once you killed Macaslan, you would try to take this territory as well. I'm sure they are all riding here as we speak."

He smiled, not the least bit bothered by my telling him that two clans were coming to kill him. "Good. Then they should arrive within the next day or two. I'm sure they were not able to keep the same pace as I did—'tis the only reason we beat them here."

It definitely wasn't the only reason, but I kept that to myself. I was eager to ask the next question on my mind. "All right, Raudrich. I've decided that I believe you. I will have your back when Callum arrives here ready to slit your throat, but I still don't understand why all of that resulted in the need for me to hang out in the stables while you said hi to Drustan."

"Lass, I've heard stories of the way Drustan treats the women he meets. If ye met him, the only way I could protect ye is to say ye are my wife, and he knows that I've none. Ye will stay here tonight, and I shall sleep in the stables. I just ask that ye lock the door when I leave so no one will disturb ye."

"Oh no, please don't do that. You must be exhausted. I really don't even know how you're standing up right now. You take the bed. I'll sleep on the floor. I won't be able to sleep at all if you sleep in the stables."

He frowned at me then moved to grab one of the blankets from the bed. "I'll sleep on the floor. Ye will sleep on the bed. That is the furthest I will compromise, aye?"

I nodded and yawned at the thought of sleep, but there were still other answers I needed. "Raudrich, why did you not say anything about the way I was dressed? It's strange to you, yes?"

He laughed and spread the blanket on the floor, far away from the bed and against the back wall of the room. "Just as I've heard stories of much that goes on in the Highlands, I've also heard stories of Cagair Castle and the strange lassies that appear there by magic, all to marry men much like myself. Aye, I thought it odd, but I simply supposed ye were one of those lassies."

"You seem to know everything. Why didn't you know about Macaslan's death until I told you?"

"I've a seer that tells me all, but she canna verra well do that while I'm in Spain. My distance from her prevented me from knowing as much as I usually do. Now, I am verra tired. Let us rest for now."

I nodded and turned toward the bed, one last thought lingering on my mind. "Okay, but what's the plan? How do we get rid of the new Laird Macaslan?"

His voice sounded sleepy as he answered, and I knew he would be asleep in a matter of seconds. "Doona ye worry about that, lass. Just *have my back* as ye said."

I laughed and collapsed into the bed as I heard him begin to snore.

CHAPTER 38

Morning took forever to arrive, as Raudrich's snoring kept me up most of the night. Not that I minded; I was glad to see him sleeping. After the number of hours he had gone without shut-eye, I was starting to worry that he was some sort of supernatural insomniac. Even if he wasn't, I was pretty sure that he and Cooper would be fast friends.

He did rise early, though, just as the sun began to peek through the window, springing up with more energy than any person had a right to have before coffee.

"Do ye hear that, Sydney?"

I sat up and listened as closely as I could. I didn't hear a thing. "Do I hear what?"

"Yer people, lass. They've arrived."

I stood and marched over to the door, opening it without hesitation to listen more clearly. Still, everything out in the hall was completely quiet. "I don't hear anything. I think maybe you need a few more hours of sleep."

"I assure ye, they are here and storming the castle at this verra moment. Are ye ready? I doona believe Callum and the others will wait long. They will be eager to find ye and the others if they believe I've held ye captive here."

"If you can hear them, you seriously got bit by some sort of weird spider as a child. Are you about to pull out a red suit or something?"

He twisted his head to the side like a confused puppy. "What?"

I shook my head. "Never mind. What are we going to do?"

He shrugged, and my eyes widened in shocked surprise.

"You don't have a plan, do you?"

"No, how could I? I doona know for sure what Callum and the others will do. All I know is that Callum and his men should have no trouble overtaking Drustan's, as I instructed my own men to abandon the castle while everyone slept last night. Just stay close to me as I follow the noise. We are sure to find them."

We crept along the long hall together, making it down the main staircase and through one of the ground level hallways before I heard anything. When Callum's voice reached my ears, I had to resist the urge to run straight for him.

"Drustan, ye know that I doona care for ye, but I am not the sort of man that believes the sins of the father should be paid by the son. If ye tell what ye've agreed to with Laird Allen, if ye tell us where he is, we willna harm ye."

Raudrich leaned forward, pushing my head toward the doorway so I could see where he was pointing.

"Do ye see the door on the back side of the dining hall? We will enter there."

I nodded in agreement as we walked around the outskirts of where Callum and his men stood with Drustan backed against a wall in the dining room. When we reached the door on the other side, Raudrich paused and looked over at me with kind eyes.

"If ye are not able to stop them in time, doona feel guilt over any of it. I will have given my life doing exactly what I was meant to do."

"What?" I looked at him nervously, confused by his words. He acted like he intended to run straight for Callum's sword. As I watched him charge through the door, drawing his blade as he went, I realized he might very well be doing just that.

I stood in the open doorway trying to understand what he meant to do, trying to watch his fast movements as he ran toward the cowering Drustan, not hesitating a moment as he plunged his sword into the young laird's stomach.

Raudrich pulled his blade out and threw it to the ground, and I knew then what he meant. He would kill Drustan to end the real evil in the room, but he wasn't willing to raise his weapon to any other.

I jerked my head toward Callum as I watched him draw his own blade and raise it over his head in anticipation of swinging it straight through Raudrich.

Screaming for him to stop, I ran directly into the path of Callum's swing and threw myself in front of Laird Allen.

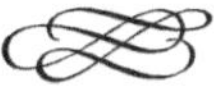

CHAPTER 39

*I*f not for the power of Morna's magic, Callum's blade would have split Sydney right down the middle. He heard her screams, even saw her running toward Laird Allen, but the witch's quick thinking was all that stopped the momentum of his downward swing. The blade left his hand suddenly, flying to the side and striking against stone as Callum fell to his knees, relief sweeping over him.

In an instant, Sydney was there, holding his face between her hands, kissing him as she wrapped her arms around him. "I'm all right. I'm all right, Callum," she whispered in his ear.

"What is the matter with ye, lass? Why would ye protect him? Has he done something to yer mind? Ye know what he's done."

"No. It wasn't him." She clung tightly to him, pushing him back as he stood and tried to lunge once more toward Laird Allen. He could see the man's lips moving, but he couldn't hear anything past Sydney's urgent cries as she continued to push him back.

"Callum, listen to me. He didn't do anything. It was Drustan—all of it."

It couldn't be true—not after finding the tartan of Allen's clan on those that attacked the Conalls. He turned and walked away from Sydney. He needed a moment to gather himself, to recover from what he'd almost done and think through what to do next. The McMillan men stood next to him at the ready, but he knew they wouldn't move without his command.

The ride here had been long and tiring—his worry over Sydney's safety so overwhelming that he'd been ready to draw blood immediately if it meant seeing her safe. But now that he knew she was, he realized there was still much he didn't know—much that didn't make sense to him. If there was any chance Sydney was right, he didn't wish to send an innocent man to his grave.

He gathered himself as he walked over to his sword, retrieving it from the ground before pointing it soundly in Laird Allen's direction. "What have ye said to Sydney to give her cause to believe ye? Yer men attacked and killed one of the Conalls only a day after they took Macaslan's head and sent me his insignia. Ye mean to take over Macaslan's territory and punish me for the part I played in yer brother's death by causing harm to those who came to my aid, aye?"

Callum watched Raudrich closely. He saw no malice in the man's eyes, no trace of evil or anger. During all his years of traveling, Callum had seen his fair share of evil men. Laird Allen, despite all evidence to the contrary, didn't strike him as one of them. It was why he had so easily trusted him the first day they met.

Laird Allen didn't respond to him right away. When he did speak, he addressed Sydney first, moving to her side and placing a hand on her shoulder so she would look at him. Callum had to refrain from running the man through with his sword out of jealousy alone.

"Are ye mad? Had I known what ye meant when ye said ye would have my back, I would've chained ye up in the stables. Ach, lass, my life is not worth ye losing yers."

Sydney swallowed and shrugged, apparently unfazed by any of it. "I'm sorry. It was just a reaction."

Callum took a step toward him, placing the point of his blade against the center of Raudrich's chest. "Ye doona need to have a hand on her to speak to her. Now answer my question."

Raudrich nodded and slowly removed his hand from Sydney's shoulder, holding up both hands in surrender. "All I told Sydney was truth. Ye are right that 'twas both my men that took Macaslan's head and that attacked the Conalls, but they dinna do so on my order. Drustan paid them off. I am ashamed to say that I doona fully have the trust of my men as of yet, though I intend to rectify that when I return to my territory."

Callum lowered his blade and motioned for those gathered around him to do the same. Much needed to be discussed, and no truth would be found if everyone continued to cling to their weapons. Only words would bring understanding among them.

I'd never seen Callum with such a stern expression on his face. It looked painful, in truth. To contort his muscles in such a way must require great effort. If he meant to hide what he was thinking, the furrowed brow, tight lip, and downcast eyes certainly did that. I couldn't tell if he wanted to scream or cry, or if he just had a massive headache.

After Raudrich explained everything, Morna insisted on shoving the same horrific liquid drops she'd snuck into my coffee down his throat just to make sure he wasn't lying. Once they had proof he was not, the tension in the room dissolved quickly.

No one would grieve the loss of Drustan Macaslan. Even his own men put up no resistance to Callum or the McMillans after they learned of his death. As far as I could tell, relief was the overwhelming emotion throughout the territory, and since the MacChristys, the McMillans, nor Laird Allen had any interest in laying claim to the land, it was up to those living in the territory to decide who controlled it.

"We canna stay here. Not even for the rest of the morning. Morna is already preparing our horses to ride out once again. She canna stand knowing that Jerry is with Grier. Raudrich claims he escorted Grier and Jerry to one of the makeshift cottages we built during the castle's repairs. Morna is ready to head that way at once."

They were the first words Callum had spoken in over half an hour, but he continued to look down as he spoke. He leaned against the ledge of a tall window, down a long hallway just off the dining room where everyone else remained. They all had instructions to leave us alone. While Callum hurried to get me away from the others, he sure took his time letting me know why.

"I know," I said. "I didn't expect for a moment that we would stay. Callum, are you all right? You look...well, I've never seen you look that way."

When he glanced up, the anger in his eyes made me wish I'd not said anything. "No, lass, I am not all right. I doona know whether to slap ye or kiss ye."

I walked over to him and gently rested my hands on his shoulders. His sort-of-threat didn't worry me for a moment. "If you choose the former, just know that you will soon thereafter have to remove my foot from your backside."

He choked on his own spit and continued to cough as he looked at me with wide eyes. For the first time, he smiled. "Ye women of the future say whatever comes into yer mind with no hesitation, even for a moment."

I shrugged and moved to run my fingers through the hair just above his ear. "Guilty."

"I would never lay foul hands on ye, but I'm so angry with ye, I can scarcely breathe."

"Angry?" I truly thought that after he knew the truth he would understand.

"Aye, angry. Ye promised me ye would not go back, and ye did. Why? Not a thing Laird Allen said gave me the answer to that."

I leaned in to hug him and continued to hold his head against me as I spoke. "Callum, Jerry was dead set on going back, and I couldn't very well stop him. I told him that I would wait for him to go quickly and come back, but he fell down the stairs, and I knew he was hurt. I couldn't leave him to bleed out in the stairwell. You'll see when we reach them. Raudrich said he required stitches."

I felt the air go out of Callum's lungs as he relaxed against me. "Ach, Sydney, I can forgive ye for that. I truly wondered if ye did it to spite me for making ye swear to stay put."

"No." I pulled back and kissed him gently. "I wouldn't do that. I'm sorry I frightened you. Did Morna know we were here? Is that how you were able to head straight for Macaslan Castle rather than go to Cagair?"

He nodded and pulled my body flat against him, kissing me with an urgency that caused my head to spin.

CHAPTER 40

"I can see ye missed one another, aye?" Raudrich teased.

I grinned sheepishly as I stood on the tips of my toes to reach high enough to hug him before he mounted his horse and left with his men.

"How can you see that?"

"Ye have a blush in yer cheeks that wasn't there before." He winked.

My hand flew up to my face.

Laughing, Raudrich said, "I was only teasing, but I see now I was right."

I smacked him gently on the arm as I clucked my tongue in disapproval. "Not cool."

He smiled and winked at me as he moved to secure his pack on the side of his horse. "Aye, lass, I'm a scoundrel, but ye must admit that ye've grown rather fond of me over these past days. Have ye not?"

It was true, and it saddened me to see him leave, knowing that his territory was so far from Cagair Castle. "I have. You are a good man, Raudrich."

He reached out and gave my arm a quick squeeze.

"And ye, lass, are one of the bonniest women I've ever had the pleasure of meeting. If ye and Callum should ever find yerself north, please do stop by."

"We will." I reached to rub his horse as he situated himself for the long ride. "So, you really don't have yourself a lady-friend, huh?"

He bobbed his head playfully toward Callum. "No, I doona. Are ye offering, lass? Have ye tired of Callum so quickly?"

I waved a dismissive hand at him as he gathered up the reins. "You know very well that's not what I was saying. It's just surprising, is all. You're very likeable."

"I doona know about that, but I hope ye are right. I've much work to do, many people to win over in my brother's territory if I am to care for the land in his stead. I hope they come to think of me as kindly as ye do."

"They will. Please send word to Cagair when you reach your destination safely. If you ever need anything, I know Callum and his men will be there for you."

He nodded and slowly turned his horse away, only to turn it back in my direction after a few steps. "Ach, I almost forgot, lass. I've carried this with me since my brother's death, but I think now perhaps the babe Nora would be better off with it than I."

He leaned over to grab something from inside his pack then handed me a small painted portrait of a man that very much resembled Raudrich and a woman that I knew had to be his wife. It was a special treasure. The fact that he was willing to give it up so Nora would have some piece of her parents touched me deeply.

"I doona know if the lassie's Ma and Da will wish for her to see her birth parents or not. They may not want her to ever know. That is their choice, but if they wish to tell her, I thought it might be nice for her to have it."

"It's more than nice. I know Jane and Adwen both. They will be happy to show this to her one day."

"It pleases me to know it. I hope that we meet again, lass. Until then, farewell."

233

CHAPTER 41

The first few days of the journey, Morna rode hard. The last day, as we approached Cagair territory, she rode like a fiend.

"Are you excited to see Jerry, or are you simply trying to get it over with?" I asked. "I really can't tell."

Morna rode a few yards ahead of Callum and me, but she twisted to look back at us as she answered. "Both. Even though I'm liable to strangle the old fool as soon as I see him, I've missed him more than ye can know. In all the years we've been married, I've not spent this long away from him. At the same time, I dread what may occur between Grier and myself."

Callum moved our horse so that it walked in step with Morna's. "Morna, I still doona know what happened between the two of ye, but I'll not allow ye to cause her harm," he said. "We've had enough violence these past weeks without ye adding to it."

She sighed before speaking. "Callum, I doona intend to harm her. She is far more likely to harm me than I am her."

"Why?" I asked. Both Morna and Jerry had been so vague about Grier for far too long. "We are bound to find out in a few minutes anyway. Just go ahead and tell us."

"Grier was my mentor. She taught me how to use magic. She guided me and cared for me during a time that was verra dark in my life. Jerry was the first man both of us ever loved."

I suspected as much the day I saw Jerry's tears on the night of his heart attack. "And he chose you?"

Morna shook her head and pointed to the small cottage in the distance. "As far as he believed, there was never any choice. Grier was his dearest friend, but I was the woman he loved. I think Grier always believed that, deep down, he loved her—that Jerry and I would run our course and then she would be here waiting. When I left and Jerry returned to the time from which he was born, she saw it as a betrayal."

"And you never saw her after that? At least, not until now?"

"No. The last words she said to either of us were those of a curse. I've been frightened of her ever since."

"Morna, I truly doona think ye've need to be scared of her," said Callum. "'Twas so long ago, she's unlikely to be the same person she was then. Are ye?" Callum fell back, allowing Morna to take the lead toward the small cottage in the distance. He knew she could sense Jerry's whereabouts.

"No, we all change with time and circumstance," Morna answered. "I shall listen, for 'tis evident to me now that perhaps that was her intention all along. She wishes to speak. So we shall."

I could make out a figure standing outside the cottage as we approached. As we neared, I knew it was Jerry. The hunch of his shadow gave him away. He waved us forward, calling out to his wife as soon as we got within hearing distance.

"Morna, lass. God, I've missed ye. Get over here."

She pulled her horse to a stop, dismounting with the grace of someone half her age, then ran the remaining distance to Jerry. For a moment, I feared she was going to jump up and wrap her legs around him—a move that was sure to send them both toppling to the ground—but she refrained, instead holding her husband so tightly that, as Callum and I rode up on our own horse, I worried Jerry would faint from lack of oxygen.

"You better let him go," I said with a laugh, only half teasing. "He's looking rather pale, Morna."

"Ach, he's always pale. I'm trying to decide if I wish to let him live or not."

Jerry laughed and pulled away from her, only to wrap his arm around her and hold her close. "Ye doona get to be mad at me. In all our years together, I dealt with one foolish errand of yers after another. This is the first time I did anything ye wished me not to do. Ye can forgive it."

Callum and I dismounted, leaving our horse to roam in the grass as we walked over to them.

"Your head looks awful, Jerry." I hugged him and reached to carefully inspect his stitches. "It looks like she did a good job, though."

"Aye, that she did, lass. My head is fine. 'Tis verra solid and large. I doona think I incurred any lasting damage."

I could sense Morna's anxiety as she pointed to the door of the cottage. "Is she in there? Why is she hiding inside?"

Jerry sighed, and I saw the same sadness in his eyes that I'd seen in them once before. "She's dying. There's not much time left for ye to speak with her."

CHAPTER 42

It's a strange thing to watch a witch die. By all outer appearances, she looked fine. The only sign of inward trouble was in her eyes. They held little spark, their color without vibrancy. Morna sat carefully on the edge of the bed as she spoke with hushed tones. Jerry stood next to us to allow them some privacy.

"What happened, Jerry?" I spoke quietly, careful not to draw attention. "Laird Allen said he saw the two of you safely here. He made no mention of Grier being ill."

"She wasna ill. She's not ill now. Witches doona die like the rest of us. They can be killed outright, but if no harm from another comes to them, their bodies only give out when they choose to release their power. Grier has started the process of releasing hers."

"Why?" I couldn't imagine anyone making such a choice, but then again, I still had so much ahead of me. How many years had Grier lived on this Earth? How many loved ones had she lost? I was certain for each of us, there would be a time when we were, indeed, ready to leave.

"Why doona ye step closer and listen?" Jerry asked. "She explains all to Morna now."

Their greeting was terse, but I saw Morna soften the longer she spoke to Grier, even reaching for her hand to hold it in her own.

"Morna, I'll not lie to ye and say I dinna mean the last words I said to ye. At the time, I did. For a year, even two, I meant them. But then, as time does, it revealed the true way of things to me. Neither of ye wanted to hurt me. Ye simply did as ye were meant to do."

Morna continued to rub the old witch's hands, speaking in a soothing tone as she did so. "What helped ye, Grier? Ye were so angry—so bitter."

Grier smiled, and for a moment the fading light in her eyes sparked back to life. "I found the one my soul was truly meant for. It was not Jerry. I knew that the moment I met my Osgar. Every day after I met him—save the last year—I spent with him by my side. The moment I gave my heart to him, I lifted the curse I placed on the two of ye."

"He died?"

Grier's voice broke as she answered, and a single, heartbreaking tear ran down her face. "Aye. I knew the day he left this world that I would follow him soon, but I couldna leave until I saw that all those I love were well and cared for. The first was Cagair, the day of the fire. The second, Jerry—I could see the trouble brewing in his heart, and I knew yer oath to never use magic on him. I made him no such promise, and I knew I had to make sure he lived for yer sake."

Grier paused and waved Jerry over so he would join them. She only resumed speaking once he sat on her other side. "Sydney and Callum were my third, though in truth I simply matched them for old time's sake. We had such fun before, dinna we, Morna?"

Morna nodded and turned to smile back at Callum and me. "Aye, we did."

"Ye and Jerry are all I've left to care for. I needed to speak with ye, needed ye to know that I still love ye both and always have. When I release my power, I'm gifting it to ye, Morna. The portal at Cagair, this domain, will be yers. Open it back or not, 'tis up to ye. Now, both of ye kiss me, for I'm weary."

Grier died beautifully, smiling and at peace.

***

"Tell me ye intend to marry her, Callum."

Callum turned his head, quickly glancing behind him to make certain Sydney couldn't hear them. He walked arm-in-arm with Morna as they made their way back to the portal so the witch could open it for the first time under her domain.

He smiled at her question. He'd thought much on it these past days. "Aye, I intend to ask her, though not yet."

"Why? Surely what we just witnessed proved that ye should hold on to those ye love as tightly as ye can. For ye will miss them more than ye can imagine once they're gone."

He squeezed Morna's arm to comfort her. "I'll be holding her tightly every night for the rest of my life, but there is none in Sydney's life she loves more than her family. I doona think it right that I ask her without knowing them first."

"Ah, Callum, ye are the wisest of men. Ye are thoughtful and kind, and she will love ye for it. Ye will invite them to the castle, then?"

"Aye. Though there's actually something I meant to speak with ye about. I doona think it fair I ask them to pay for their flight..."

Morna interrupted him mid-sentence. "Doona worry about that at all, lad. I've some magical cards that will work just fine but cost nothing."

Callum laughed, but he would gladly accept Morna's help. He had little in the way of twenty-first century funds. "Do ye not consider that fraud?"

"O'course 'tis fraud, but I'm a witch not a saint. Do ye wish me to help or not?"

He hurried to reassure her. "I do—verra much so. I also wish to seek yer counsel on another matter."

Morna knew his question before he asked it. "Aye, lad. Ye must tell her family, though let's go about it in a better way than we did with Sydney, aye? If I know the lass, she willna be willing to give up her job at the castle, which means ye will both be living verra much in two different times. It will be so much easier on her if her family knows."

He agreed. He just didn't know how to go about telling them. It was such an ordeal with every new person that knew. "How do we tell them?"

"What about this, lad? I would love to be there when ye asked her, anyway. Why doona ye send word to me when ye know for certain when her family is arriving, and Jerry and I will come back up for the weekend. I shall give them a little something just to open their minds a bit and make them more accepting to the news. If ye wish, I'll even tell them myself, make certain they know and believe it before Sydney even knows they've arrived."

Callum smiled as they reached the top of the portal. He wouldn't have been able to come up with a better plan himself. "I knew I loved ye for a reason, Morna. Now open up the portal so we may call this day good and done."

agair Castle—*Present Day—One Month Later*

"Are ye certain ye can keep her distracted until I come back for her?"

Callum didn't know what he was thinking leaving his brother in charge of keeping watch over Sydney, but as busy as everyone was making preparations, Adwen was really the only choice he had.

"Aye. I already know what to tell her. She'll enjoy the morning alone in yer castle, I'm sure of it."

Callum didn't have time to worry about it further. Morna was speaking with Sydney's parents and sister at that very moment. Once she finished, he would have a very important conversation with her father.

"Fine. Then go before she finishes her run and realizes I've come forward through the portal. I doona know how long 'twill be before I'm ready, but doona let her pass through that stairwell until I return."

Adwen gave his word and ran off toward the portal, leaving him to gather his nerves before he went to check on Morna's success in letting them in on the magical truth.

He'd already met Sydney's family and had visited with them every moment during the ride from the airport. Callum thought them to be as kind, lovely, and full of life as Sydney, and he couldn't wait to call them family. Assuming, of course, her father granted him permission to ask her in the first place.

Cautiously, he peered into the sitting room to listen in on Morna's words. She must have sensed his presence for she turned immediately, smiling widely as she waved him into the room.

"Come here, Callum. I was just telling Sydney's family all about how Sydney is spending the morning in the seventeenth century. They think it is lovely."

Callum walked up behind Morna's chair where he could see their expressions. They didn't appear spelled or hypnotized. They just looked as if it were a normal, everyday thing of which to speak.

He looked directly at Sydney's father. "Do ye really? And ye think it possible, then?"

Her father, Gary, shrugged and nodded. "Well, it's certainly surprising, but if they can put men on the moon, I don't know why they couldn't put them in the past. I can't wait to try it out myself."

Callum directed his attention to Sydney's mother. "What about ye?"

"Sydney's always been about living outside the box, so it doesn't surprise me that she's ended up living with a bunch of magical beings."

He felt the need to clarify. "Oh, we're not magical. 'Tis only Morna. We simply make use of her magic with a great deal of frequency."

"Well, whatever. As long as you treat my baby with the respect and love she deserves, I truly don't care."

Finally, he looked at Liv. Out of the three of them, she looked the most skeptical. "I'd think it was a lot more awesome if she told me herself. She tells me everything."

Callum smiled, and he knew then that it wasn't only her father he needed to ask. They all loved Sydney so much, and she would want each of their blessings.

"Might I ask ye all a question? I invited ye here not only because I wished to meet ye, but also because I am verra much in love with Sydney. If ye all grant me yer permission, I would love to ask her to marry me this night."

The deafening silence that followed his request told him that Morna had indeed only altered their ability to easily accept the possibility of magic. All of their other opinions and thoughts were just as they would have always been.

His nerves grew until Liv stood and pointed at both her parents while she smiled widely. "I told you that's what was going on. Yes! I finally get to be in a wedding."

An overwhelming blessing by both of Sydney's parents followed Liv's excitement, and as Callum moved in to hug them, he feared his heart might burst from happiness.

CHAPTER 44

*1*650

I returned from my morning run to find Callum gone from the castle and Adwen standing outside our window in his stead.

"Good morning to ye, Sydney. Do ye mind coming down here a moment?"

I leaned out of the high window to answer him. "Yeah, sure. Hang on just a second and let me change. Where's Callum?"

"Oh, he traveled down to the village for a few hours. Anne asked me to come through and talk to ye."

"Okay. Just a minute."

I hurried to dress and ran down the castle's many steps two at a time. When I stepped outside, Adwen was pacing nervously.

"Is she worried about breakfast or something? It's a Saturday, so I figured she wanted it a little later. I was just about to come through."

He held up a hand to stop me.

"No, nothing like that. In fact, she told me to come and tell ye not to come to the kitchen this morning. Ye have the day off."

Alarm bells went off in my head immediately. There was absolutely no reason why I should have the day off. "What are you talking about? There's no way Anne said that." I tried to brush past him, but he stepped in my path once more.

"Aye, she did. Ye see, she's hosting a party this morning for a group of ladies she knows, and she..." He paused and scratched his head, as if he couldn't find the word. "Ach, what is the word ye use when ye pay someone to bring in food?"

"A caterer?" I screeched the word at him. "She hired a caterer? Tell me you're joking."

Adwen smiled, clearly not picking up on my escalating anger. "Aye, a caterer. She did. She thought ye might want the morning off."

I placed both hands on my hips as I braced to charge him. "Let me be sure I'm getting this right. Not only is Anne having a party that she didn't invite me to attend, but she also didn't think my cooking was good enough for it?"

Adwen nodded, seemingly satisfied with himself. "Aye, precisely."

"I call foul. You're lying."

His smile vanished. "No. I'm not lying, and ye canna go through. Ye will disturb their party if ye do. It will only embarrass ye both."

I turned my head from side to side as I tried to gauge the best path I could take to get around him. He was big and fast. I would have to go through him.

"I don't care. I embarrass myself pretty regularly anyway."

I ran straight for him, anticipating that he would grab on to me even before he did so. I waited until he lifted me high enough that both feet were off the ground, and then I jabbed my knee hard into his stomach.

He cried out as he released me, clutching his middle and leaning forward.

"Sorry. You gave me no choice."

I ran to the portal and started screaming Anne's name even before I passed through. If Adwen had lied, I wanted to know exactly what was going on. If he hadn't, Anne and I were about to have one heck of a conversation.

"Anne. Anne." I continued calling her name as I made it into the twenty-first century and ran up the stairs and into the castle.

There were people standing in the foyer when I pushed open the main doors. In my shock, it took me a moment to realize who they were.

My parents.

Tears of joy welled up in my eyes as I rushed to greet them.

CHAPTER 45

"Mom? Dad? Liv?" I could scarcely believe it even as I hugged and kissed them. "What are you doing here? I talked to you three days ago, and you were at home. You didn't say anything about this."

My mother wrapped her arm around my shoulder and gestured to Callum as I looked over at him with teary eyes. "Callum invited us. It's been arranged for weeks now. He wanted to surprise you. He even picked us up at the airport this morning. He's been telling us all about what his duties are as laird and the difference between this Cagair and the Cagair of his own time."

"What?" At her mention of that, I was certain I was dreaming.

Callum nodded. "They know, lass. Morna told them. She helped them...she helped them to understand...to accept it."

I pulled away from my mother for just a moment so I could speak with Callum out of earshot. I grabbed his hands and led him a few steps away. "Morna's here?"

"Aye. She and Jerry arrived just after yer parents. She agreed to help me so that the knowing wouldna be so hard for them."

I moved to kiss him. I didn't know if I'd ever been so happy. "Callum, this is wonderful. You can't know what it means to me—

to have them here, to have them know the truth—it's everything. I love you so much."

He kissed my brow and held my face in his hands as he spoke. "I love ye, too, lass. I've a few things I must attend to today. Please spend the day with yer family. I'll meet ye for dinner."

The mention of food reminded me of Adwen, and I guiltily bit my lower lip.

"Callum, you might want to go and check on your brother first. I sort of...well, I think I knocked the air out of him."

Callum stepped away from me in surprise. "What did ye do that for?"

"He told me that Anne was having a party and I wasn't invited. Plus, he said she'd hired a caterer to feed them. It made me angry, and he wouldn't let me through, so I took him out of commission to get by him."

Clearly exasperated, Callum ran his hand through his hair. "Ach, I knew he was the wrong person to send to distract ye, though he wasn't lying about everything. I did have Anne hire a caterer for the week. I dinna want ye cooking while yer family was here. I wanted ye to be able to enjoy every moment with them."

I huffed, feeling guiltier by the second. "I guess I owe Adwen quite the apology."

"Ye can do that later, lass. I'll see to him now. Go and enjoy yer family. I'll see ye at dinner."

The food, much to my chagrin, was delicious and the company so wonderful that I didn't think my heart could hold any more happiness. Callum moved everyone into the sitting room after dinner where he had a large fire going and furniture arranged so we could all gather around it.

Conversation flowed easily—though I only vaguely listened to most of it. I was too distracted by my thoughts of Callum—by my overwhelming gratitude and disbelief at his thoughtfulness.

It was only when he spoke up for the first time during the conversation that I listened. "Aiden, why doona ye tell us about the first moment ye knew ye loved Anne?"

It seemed an odd question for Callum to ask him, but I found myself curious as to the answer. I knew they were both crazy about one another, but as much time as I'd spent with Anne, her relationship with Aiden had never come up.

Aiden happily obliged him.

"We were at university together. She came here to study Gaelic, though in truth, I know she only came here to study Gaelic men. We were in three classes together our first semester, and I always made a point of sitting behind her so I could watch the light bounce off her golden hair. One day, about midway through the semester, she turned around and said..." He stopped and pointed to Anne so she would finish.

She smiled and snuggled in close to him. "I turned to him and said, 'My favorite flowers are lilies. I'll have a vase and some water ready for them when you come and pick me up at eight.'"

Everyone laughed as he leaned in to kiss her. "I knew then I would marry her."

Callum pointed to Adwen and asked the same question.

"The moment Jane kissed Orick just to silence me, she owned my heart completely. I knew it because I'd never been so jealous in my life."

"Orick, what about ye?"

Callum continued going down the line of couples. It became clear to me that he intended for each to share. Sap that I am, I loved every minute of it.

Orick reached up to brush his wife's red hair from her shoulder, as he spoke only to her.

"I loved ye before I met ye. I saw ye in a window and knew then ye were the only lassie that would ever rule my heart."

My own parents went next, and theirs was a story I already knew. Dad was touring Italy with his then girlfriend, though she left him for another man in Rome, and he continued his trip without her. When he returned to the States, he returned with my mom.

Finally, it was Jerry and Morna's turn. Theirs was the story I was most eager to hear.

Jerry reached for Morna, placing a hand upon her knee as he spoke. "I canna say for sure, for I'm fair certain she spelled me to love her against my will."

Everyone laughed except Morna, and she hurried to set the record straight. "Hogwash. It took ye the better part of a year to convince me to even look twice at ye. I can tell ye precisely when ye first fell in love with me. 'Twas the moment we first danced."

Jerry pulled Morna's hand up to his mouth to kiss it before speaking to Callum. "And what about ye, lad? I believe ye are the only fellow left."

I twisted so I could look at him. I was quite curious to hear the answer myself. He faced me, smiled, and then stood. "I'll tell ye, but first I must remove what has been poking me in my side all day."

He bent to one knee as I noticed the ring in his hand. My sudden intake of breath caused my lip to tremble. "Callum..."

Before I could say more, he said, "No, lass. Let me speak, for 'tis my turn to say when I knew I loved ye. The answer is, I doona know. I canna think of one instance, one word, or one glance with which ye captured my heart. Ye dinna enter my life as a strike of lightning. Instead, ye are the gentlest of rains that slowly and surely brings the flowers to life.

"I liked ye, I cared for ye, from the start. But the loving of ye, that has built slowly, day by day, hour by hour. I doona think I'm near finished. I'll love ye more each day until I take my last breath, and if ye'll have me, 'tis exactly what I intend to do."

He held up the ring—its silver band encompassing a green

stone so lovely and large I feared its weight on my finger—and said the words that made more tears spill from my eyes.

"Marry me, Sydney. Marry me, and I will never stop ye from being the lass ye wish to be, whether it be in this time or my own. We can manage both. Will ye?"

"Of course I will." I kissed him between sobs of joy, and my hand shook terribly as he moved to place the ring on my finger.

If my months at Cagair had taught me anything, it was how to live. I didn't understand how little of that I'd been doing until I passed through Cagair's doors and stairwells.

So many people, so many emotions, had filled these halls the past months—fear, anger, sadness, grief—but there were also great moments of laughter, joy, and love.

As I melted into Callum's arms, with so many of those I knew and loved gathered around celebrating his proposal, I knew that even though trouble, sadness, and grief were sure to come again— as long as there was love, there was life.

And in the end, everything would be okay as long as we stood at each other's side.

Morna & Jerry's Home

Morna crawled into bed next to her husband, and she didn't think she'd ever been so happy to do so.

"Jerry, promise me that we doona have to leave this house at least until Christmas. This year has tired me to no end."

Her husband's laugh, old yet strong, tickled her neck as he snuggled in closer to her.

"'Tis fine by me, lass. Ye are the one always dragging me about so."

"Hmm..." She started to drift, content to sleep with Jerry's arms around her, but woke again at the sound of his voice.

"Morna, might I ask ye something? Ye dinna really speak true at Cagair—when Callum asked when I knew I loved ye. Why?"

She pursed her lips, memories of the time so long ago flooding her mind.

"I dinna lie to them completely. We did dance often, did we

not? What I told them was all they needed to hear for now. The rest can wait for another day."

That day would come soon, she knew. The memories simply wouldn't stay put any longer. It was time for her story—the real story—to be told.

THE END

Thank you for reading *Morna's Vow*. I hope you enjoyed it! If you did...

1. Help other people find this book by writing a review.
2. Go to www.bethanyclaire.com and sign up for my newsletter to be notified of new releases.
3. Visit me on Facebook at www.facebook.com/bethanyclaire.
4. Visit my website: www.bethanyclaire.com

BETHANY CLAIRE is a USA Today bestselling author of swoon-worthy, Scottish romance and time travel novels. Bethany loves to immerse her readers in worlds filled with lush landscapes, hunky Scots, lots of magic, and happy endings.

She has two ornery fur-babies, plays the piano every day, and loves Disney and yoga pants more than any twenty-something really should. She is most creative after a good night's sleep and the perfect cup of tea. When not writing, Bethany travels as much as she possibly can, and she never leaves home without a good book to keep her company.

If you want to read more about Bethany or if you're curious about when her next book will come out, please visit her website at: www.bethanyclaire.com, where you can sign up to receive email notifications about new releases.

ACKNOWLEDGMENTS

J.J. Archer, Mom, Maegan, Karen Corboy, Elizabeth Halliday, Vivian Nwankpah, Johnetta Ivey, Pamela Oviatt, and Rori Bumgarner: A special thanks to each of you for helping me get this book out to readers. I am more thankful for you than you will ever know.